Long Jetty Short Stories 2

Also by Sean Crawley and published by Ginninderra Press

Dead People Don't Make Jam

Long Jetty Short Stories 1

Sean Crawley

Long Jetty
Short Stories 2

Long Jetty Short Stories 2
ISBN 978 1 76109 400 2

Cover image: Sean Crawley

First published 2022 by
GINNINDERRA PRESS
PO Box 3461 Port Adelaide 5015
www.ginninderrapress.com.au

Contents

Circa 2020

Around this time, it became inevitable that no matter how advanced we pretended to be, how sophisticated and technologically savvy, the world was unmistakably, well and truly, on its way to hell in a handbasket.

The big question was how to make the best of it. Sure, there were some people who still wanted to save the world, and there were others who were doing everything in their power to speed up collapse, but the bulk of us just wanted to get on with human stuff as best we could.

This big machine we had created, the latest iteration of human civilisation – who knows what future historians will call it – became so complex and unwieldy that it didn't matter which lever you pulled, the damn thing was spinning out of control, large chunks breaking off, the whole shebang destined to crash and burn. The exact trajectory and time duration of the death spiral was uncertain, like so many other things, circa 2020. And this uncomfortable certainty that there was no certainty, this not knowing why, where, what, when, how, or who, was perhaps the greatest challenge for those of us wanting to enjoy whatever was left. How to sing and dance and love each other in times of uncertainty. Be it a bang or a whimper, just how could one go out in style?

Bucking the general trend, Frank Admission was doing it on his ear. Like some others, he had seen the writing on the wall long before. And, unlike some, he didn't become a prepper. He figured that all the energy and time needed to design and build bunkers, and then stock them with food and weapons and whatever else might be needed, would take one away from the pleasures and joys of living in the present. Besides, what if the end of the world, inevitable as it was, took a hundred years or more? All that prepping for what? Nothing?

Everything has a beginning, middle and end. No one chooses when they are born.

Frank spent his time just watching the planet and its inhabitants. Not painting it, or photographing it, not blogging about it or reading about it, just watching, and smiling a lot.

Admittedly, Frank had done his fair share of writing. His science fiction crime novels were credited as the prototypes for a whole new genre. Bookshops ended up having to make new signage and allocate dedicated shelves. It was a well known commercial fact that every book needed to be classified. Sci-cri became all the rage. It proved to be a cash cow for Frank and the litany of copycat writers who followed. Publishing houses, who for many years completely ignored Frank and his attempts at literary fiction, ended up competing fiercely to sign him. He was hot property, bankable.

You see, literary fiction was not economically viable unless you had a name in literary fiction, they said. Talk about a catch-22. (Ironically, a work of literary fiction itself.) The globalised, industrialised, digitised civilisation of the twenty-first century was littered with catch-22s. 'You have to have money to make money' being the most common, and most frustrating. Money did make the world go round. And the way it was distributed meant there were not many happy campers.

Frank switched from literary fiction to commercial fiction, also known as genre fiction, not from any desire to become lauded as a published author, but from sheer financial need. Several acrimonious marriage break-ups had wreaked havoc on his mediocre wealth portfolio. Even his future financial fecundity, locked up in superannuation, had been quarantined by several parties. And as all those trillions of dollars of workers' savings started to disappear, Frank smiled and pondered whether karma was just as real as any other established law of physics. The law of entropy was certainly wreaking havoc all over the planet, circa 2020.

Once Frank paid off all his debts to society, he stopped writing sci-cri. He'd had sufficient fun inventing future worlds filled with undesirable characters willing and able to exploit hitherto unknown opportunities for theft, fraud and wanton violence. His menagerie of yet-to-be-born sleuths, such as the sexy Asperger-afflicted police officer Fiona Infinity, and the even sexier all-pervasive virtual algorithm AI-PI v6.4, became household names. His trilogy *The Stink,* volumes I, II and III, based on the brazen theft of gas from Uranus, was claimed by numerous critics to be the penultimate archetypal masterpiece of sci-cri. Most readers, though, millions of them as it turned out, simply enjoyed Frank's cleverly constructed whodunits which explored, by rocket or time machine, the universal themes of love, tragedy, politics, and comedy. Of course, there was also the industry-required smattering of sci-cri tropes, most of which Frank himself had invented.

Frank Admission played the game. He fulfilled contractual requirements. He did YouTube and podcast interviews, and made appearances at writing festivals. His face appeared on every hardcover dust jacket and every paperback back cover. He even had a blog and an Instagram account. The literary world which had rejected his earlier non-commercial, non-genre writing now adored the new Wonder from Down Under.

Upon retirement, Frank dropped his nom de plume, changed his address and seriously considered cosmetic surgery. He wished to be able to walk the streets with anonymity. The compulsory mask-wearing was a godsend.

Sunrises and sunsets were the easy parts of the day, circa 2020. You could just sit and watch the dance of Earth and Sun. Early mornings, the brain not yet soaked in the worries of the world. A new start – beginnings, possibilities, plans and ideas forming. And the sun, rising, warming, illuminating, while birds sang oblivious to the ending of the world as we knew it. Late afternoon, day is done, all the mayhem meaningless, nothing mattered any more, tomorrow another day. And the sky, as always, reddened, oranged, purpled – a spectrum of peace and restfulness. Winds abated, sleep not far off.

It was the middle of the day that was problematic. Especially when jobs and growth were off the agenda. What to do? What to think? How can one unlearn everything we were conditioned to believe without question? How can I cope with the uncertainty of everything? Shouldn't I be busy with all this time off? I should be creative at least.

What a fantastic time to be alive, thought Frank. And how easy is it to type 2020? Dum dum dum dummm. Beethoven's 5th. Two fingers.

Yes, Frank still wrote. A journal, to be buried, when the time came, in the backyard. A history for future historians who will wonder, *what were they thinking*?

The end of the world? You've got to be kidding, wrote Frank. How histrionic. How anthropocentric. The end of aeroplanes and the internet maybe. Look at the birds and the fish and the trees and the sunrises and sunsets. You've got to laugh.

And Frank did just that.

In the mornings and in the evenings, Frank donned his mask and headed out into the world. His public face covered. The so-called 'world' ending. He had never been as happy and joyous. He had his old name back, another mask. No one knew he was a famous writer, that he was the man who created the fictional worlds they read in books and watched on screens. No one pestered him. Will there be another season of *The Stink*? A sequel, or a spin-off perhaps? We need something to distract us from the ending of the world, please. Frank knew all too well how his creative writing fitted into the scheme of things – mere distraction for the fearful masses. He didn't care. In the middle of his life, he did what he had to, wrote books that would sell. Some would say he sold out. It didn't matter what people said. The 'world' was ending. Ending like everything ends.

The man once known as Frank Admission was living his own sunset. He sat and he watched, he typed 2020 with gusto into his electronic journal, and he smiled.

The Consultant

After a day's work, Thomas likes to pour himself a wine and watch *Brainiac* on television. It's how he unwinds from all the craziness and bullshit he has endured from precisely eight thirty a.m. to five p.m. Apparently, there is a book, hidden somewhere at his workplace, into which late arrivals and early departures are recorded.

Work is a nightmare enacted during daylight hours.

Home is a sanctuary, a wellness retreat, a rehabilitation centre.

What is it about *Brainiac*? Thomas asks himself occasionally. He does enjoy the questions, especially the general knowledge ones. It reminds him of school, where he did quite well. Somehow, Thomas has a memory that ranks well above average. He can be exposed to certain facts and they stick in his head. Once, after a barrage of aptitude testing done by an HR recruitment agency, Thomas was advised that his results ranked in the highest percentile. There's a certain sense of self-worth that comes from getting answers right.

'What is the Italian word for "red"?'

'*Rosso*,' answers Thomas.

The candidate on TV pauses with a grimace, then passes.

On *Brainiac*, the contestants are called candidates. They are in the running for the title of Australia's #1 Brainiac, which comes with a military-looking medal that is pinned by the host onto the upper-body garment worn by the eventual winner of the Final of Finals. There is no cash, no whitegoods appliances, no holidays to tropical locations, no prizes at any stage of the competition. Just weekly winners who get called back for the semi-finals and major finals at the back end of each season. It's all about the title, *Brainiac*. Surely no one cares about the medal?

The show airs Monday to Friday at six p.m.

There is no way Thomas would apply to be a candidate. For a start, what would his special expert subject be? It appears you can choose any obscure realm of knowledge, like the person tonight whose subject area is the Beach Boys' album *Pet Sounds*. Admittedly, Thomas does know some albums from his youth where he could name every song, and who wrote it, and recall the lyrics. But, there is no way he could name producers, recording studios, chart rankings and so on. And that is exactly the sort of minutiae they ask.

Thomas does actually have expert knowledge about one special area – Personality Disorders. But that is related to his livelihood. You get asked for your livelihood when introduced on the show. Thomas can't recall ever hearing anyone's special expert subject area being related to their job title. There must be a rule which stipulates that special subject areas must be areas of interest and not related to occupations that generate incomes that provide the candidate with a livelihood – or something like that.

Thomas is a psychotherapist specialising in Cluster B Personality Disorders. He works in a division of public health. It is insanely bureaucratic and run by a director who is a malignant narcissist. Her cronies are classic enablers who do stuff like keeping written records of the staff who arrive late or leave early. The culture of blame and micromanagement is so intense that the consequent staff turn over creates a wind that will blow right through you. Most of the 'clinicians' who work there are secretly planning to escape by opening up their own private practices. Thomas has no such dream. He is able to survive in this toxic workplace environment only by reminding himself that if he hangs in for five more years, he will have paid off his mortgage and have just enough super to retire. In the meantime, he gets home, drinks wine and watches *Brainiac* before cooking himself dinner.

On the weekends, Thomas rejuvenates by tending to and propagating orchids and bromeliads in his shade house out the back. Every now and then, he reactivates his online dating account. Every now and then, he deactivates the same account after a string of disastrous coffee dates.

Maybe I could use Australian native orchids as my special expert subject area?

But he dismisses the thought as quickly as it pops into his mind. There is no way he is going on national television.

'The fingerprints of humans share many characteristics with which marsupial?'

'Koala,' snaps Thomas.

Thomas hypothesises that his failure to find a mate is directly related to both his livelihood and area of special interest.

Everyone asks what you do for a living; coffee dates are no exception. When he answers, 'Psychotherapist,' he watches intently for their reactions.

He imagines their worry.

Who is this fellow? He calls himself Thomas? What's wrong with Tom? Mr Double-shot Cappuccino! And regular milk? No wonder he's chubby! Claims he's a psychotherapist. I bet he's analysing my every word and gesture.

And he does. He invariably finds signs and symptoms. Tick, tick tick, the DSM-5 criteria clear in his photographic mind.

Everyone asks what you do outside of work. When he mentions his orchid and bromeliad hobby, he detects the internal squirming of women who obviously want a more rugged male.

To his credit, Thomas accepts responsibility that his spectacular failure with women is as much about himself as it is about the women he meets at various cafés.

'According to Brian Wilson, what album by the Beatles inspired *Pet Sounds?*'

'*Rubber Soul*,' Thomas answers as quickly as the candidate on the telly – a middle-aged merchandise assistant wearing a Hawaiian shirt.

The job titles are another aspect of the show which Thomas loves. This particular fellow, with a head full of Beach Boys trivia, probably works at K-Mart or JB Hi-Fi. Merchandise assistant, what else could that be? Sometimes the job is obvious, like baker, for example. Bakers bake, they get up early, they work with flour and large ovens. But mostly, the titles for people's livelihoods are obfuscating jargon.

Facilities coordinator, territory business manager, technical officer, acquisition specialist. What a lark.

Patricia, the receptionist at the Division of Mental Health Services where Thomas works, has a sign on her counter which reads, 'Director of First Impressions'. Thomas has seen Patricia's profile on his on-again-off-again dating site, and he suspects she has seen his. Nothing has been said by either of them. And nothing will. Too close to home, they would argue. They actually get on well. After Thomas had been working in the division for several months, after Patricia assessed that he was not, and never would be, one of the inner circle, Patricia began to speak openly to Thomas about certain people and certain goings-on. It was how Thomas found out about the book with the list of late arrivals and early departures. And he noted that Patricia's judgement of the boss as being a bully, and therefore insecure, was very astute.

Maybe when I retire, if Patricia is still single, I will ask her out.

Thomas has had workplace relationships before and has concluded they are ineluctably problematic. His last fling, Alison, at the Davidson Clinic where he worked as a family counsellor, ended so badly he resigned and took on this present position in public health.

No, Patricia is definitely off-limits.

The final contestant is called up to centre stage. Name, Roberto Dattoli. Livelihood, consultant. Special expert subject, British Military Aircraft of World War II.

Consultant? What the…?

Roberto is a heavy-set man wearing a navy blue polo shirt, denim shorts that extend just below the knee, black crew socks and a pair of cheap runners. He looks like the blokes who work on the dock out the back of Thomas's local Woolworths supermarket. All he needs is a hi-vis vest and a cigarette tucked behind his ear.

Consultant! Ha, love this show.

Ultimately, it's the candidates that Thomas likes most about

Brainiac. Such a mixed bag. There are males and females, older people, younger people, a range of skin colours and body sizes. Then there are the clothes they wear. Wondering why Roberto has chosen to wear what he has worn for his big debut on national television is delicious food for thought. It certainly takes one's mind off work. Then there are the personalities projected by the candidates in the exchange of chit-chat with the host before they get grilled on their special expert subject. There are extroverts and introverts, smiley people and the serious types, people you would like to meet and those who you know you'd run a mile from.

Roberto presents as a quiet and humble man. Thomas likes him. How cool to not dress up at all. He imagines Roberto as a reliable and solid friend. You know, salt of the earth type. Though his job title irks Thomas.

Consultant? Are you an IT consultant? A financial consultant? Come on Roberto, what do you actually do?

'Which World War II two-seater RAF fighter had all its armament in a power-operated dorsal turret?'

Thomas has no idea.

Roberto answers with a question, 'Is it the Mohawk?'

He is wrong. In Roberto's special subject area, he scores just three correct answers. In the general knowledge round, he does better and scores a six. After the first rounds, he is last in fourth position and has to exit the stage. It is then that Thomas notices the limp and, looking closer, he sees that Roberto's left leg is a prosthetic.

An infrequent but familiar sensation runs through the body of Thomas. Empathy? Pity? Compassion? Feeling sorry for someone? Though a psychotherapist, Thomas is unable to accurately articulate what he himself is feeling. His work is clinical and focuses on others and not himself. All he knows is that a cocktail of neurotransmitters has just been squirted into his brain and this has triggered a wave of human emotion that disrupts the usual joy he experiences while watching *Brainiac*.

So much for unwinding after work.

Thomas finishes his wine and heads to the kitchen in the add break for a second glass. In the next round of *Brainiac*, the remaining three candidates are all asked the same set of questions. The questions are a mix of general knowledge and easier special expert subject questions. The questions are multiple choice. The candidates stand at their individual podiums and lock in their answers with a button.

Thomas is distracted now. He can't concentrate on the questions or enjoy the show. He can't stop thinking about Roberto. There is this strange desire to reach out and comfort him in some way. It's something about the combination of Roberto's clothing, his lack of success with the *Brainiac* questions, the man's quiet and unassuming personality, and the fact he has only one leg. Something in Thomas has been pierced. But at the same time, Thomas feels naive, patronising and embarrassingly pathetic. Rational Thomas is quite sure that Roberto is doing fine. He imagines the man going home to a loving family. He imagines Roberto being good at, and liking, his work as a consultant, whatever that may be, and being well liked by his colleagues and clients.

And then the shame hits. The self-loathing. The remembrance of past mistakes. The admission of weaknesses. The realisation he himself is a man who evaluates and advises his damaged clients, yet is incapable of applying his knowledge and skills to help himself. A man alone, watching television and drinking wine to end his day of tedium. An existential angst that no amount of wine or *Brainiac* will ever dissolve.

There are a couple of things Thomas does know from his work as a psychotherapist. One is that you shouldn't lie to yourself. There is no way I am going to be able to do this for five more years, he confesses to himself. The other is that unless you do something, nothing will change.

'Come on, wear it. I dare you!' says Patricia, referring to the *Brainiac* medal.

'I'm not even sure I want to go,' says Thomas.

It is the thirty-year anniversary of the Division of Mental Health.

A big do at a local function centre. Present and past staff are invited. Patricia and Thomas are past staff, happily so. They resigned from their jobs not long after they connected online.

The night Thomas watched Roberto on *Brainiac*, he 'nudged' Patricia on the dating site. What the heck, he thought. Then, on a roll, he registered to be a candidate on *Brainiac*.

Thomas's special subject area was Australian Native Orchids, his stated his livelihood as consultant. He won the season. And it turns out that Patricia loves gardening, is a whizz at managing and being the Director of First Impressions at the private practice which they run from Thomas's house, now their home.

Every now and then, Thomas streams the episode of *Brainiac* with Roberto Dattoli. And though so much has changed since he first watched it, he still can't shake the desire of wanting to meet the man. He'd love to give him a big thank you hug and say, 'Guess what, Roberto? I'm a consultant, just like you!'

March–April 2020

Wednesday, 18 March 2020

6.14 a.m.

…everything is shutting down. Time to write? Yeah, write.

Thursday, 19 March 2020

6.54 a.m.

Apparently, now is the time to get on with all those creative ideas that we've had bubbling away on that back burner in our brain. Because apparently, up till now we've been so occupied by sprinting flat out in the human race to get ahead, that there has been no spare time or energy left over for pursuits such as writing or sketching or nurturing a garden or baking a sourdough loaf of bread.

Apparently, we are so programmed to achieve, that even in lockdown, or self-isolation, we still need to be productive!

Or what about being nice to others, and reconnecting with family and loved ones? Apparently, we haven't been doing enough of that while we've been working, or searching for work, to keep a roof over our heads and food on the table.

Now, if creative pursuits or human relationships aren't your thing, apparently, according to fifty squillion emails in my Junk folder, the winding down of the rat race is the perfect time to make a small fortune with bitcoin! Apparently, even while a microscopic life form is teaching us an important lesson about the dangers of exponential growth, the economy still trumps everything else.

How about we just have a rest? Put up the feet and shift the nervous and endocrine systems into neutral. Do that for as long as required. Let our own minds and bodies decide when we're ready to go again. Apparently, that could be good for our health.

Friday, 20 March 2020

5.07 a.m.

What we talk about when we talk about the economy.

Money. Which is fair enough since money is the ticket to everything that has been monetised, and virtually everything has been monetised.

In Australia, as in many other nations, real estate has been monetised. Our current government defends the right of anyone, including the quiet mum and dad investors, to build wealth by investing in real estate. Not only do they defend that right, essentially a right to build wealth upon the backs of those less fortunate, that subclass we call renters, the government actually encourages it with tax breaks. Now in a crisis, the renters who lose their employment will become even more vulnerable.

It's little wonder that many of us are welcoming the looming recession. Australia's twenty-eight years of continuous economic growth have benefited the few and not the many. This growth has damaged the environment so terribly we don't even know if it is reparable. Unfettered capitalism has created more billionaires and a greater divide between the haves and the have-nots. And this is in Australia, the nation which claims to be some sort of egalitarian paradise. There is enormous wealth in this country, and we know who has it. It's time for a redistribution. At the very least, nobody should become homeless because they can't pay their rent or mortgage.

The lack of any real socialism in action in the Western world for such a long time makes me angry and sad, and lamenting what could have been.

It's little wonder that people panic buy and hoard. For goodness sake, the economic system in this country is all about looking after oneself. Our Prime Minister repeats, 'A fair go for those who have a go.'

Article 25: We all have the right to enough food, clothing, housing and healthcare for ourselves and our families. We should have access to support if we are out of work, ill, elderly, disabled, widowed, or can't earn a living for reasons outside of our control. An expectant mother and her baby should both receive extra care and support. All children should have the same rights when they are born. (Universal Declaration of Human Rights)

Sunday, 22 March 2020

6.11 a.m.
Well, here I sit in my office, while outside a virus is changing the world as we know it.

How much will the world change after Covid-19?

What will become irrelevant? What will become essential? What will writers write? What will I write?

An idea for a novel is swirling around in the old brain pool. I am assessing it in the light of this new day. Rationally, I know the pandemic will pass, and people will still want stories, and when it passes, I predict the world will, unfortunately, go back to business as usual. Most people will not want the world to go back to business as usual, but as usual, it won't be the majority who get their way, it will be the ruling classes who get their way. This may sound a bit defeatist, and I hope I am wrong in regard to how the world will readjust itself after the pandemic, but the wealthy, and thus powerful, will not surrender their positions that easily. So it'll be back to a neo-liberal reality. The masses doing the hard yards while the wealthy get a free ride. The reality being that economic growth flows up and doesn't, as they want us to believe, trickle down.

Monday, 23 March 2020

7.23 a.m.
I'm not sure what I am going to be allowed to do tomorrow.

Things are changing rapidly.

There are new rules for Australia everyday and then there are the rules for NSW.

I'll turn on the radio at eleven a.m. to get an update. Maybe find out if I'll be working later in the week. And hoping that walking to the beach for a swim is not banned, decided to be NON-ESSENTIAL.

Tuesday, 24 March 2020

6.34 a.m.
Please note:

From today, any person you spot, out and about, dressed in Active Wear, is not going to, or coming from, the gym.

Saturday, 28 March 2020

7.07 a.m.
As the world hunkers down, the optimists call for the rebirth of the good old things that we used to do before the world went bat-shit crazy over capitalism.

Learn something, like a new language or how to play a musical instrument. We are going to need music, and not the manufactured pop that's been shoved down our throats this century but real music, live and in your face and played by human hands and mouths. Pull out that box of paints and those pre-primed canvases that were left untouched while the world called upon you for more and more hours and new qualifications and a dedication that drained every last creative impulse.

Since I recently came out as an author, people have been saying to me, 'Well, this whole corona virus thing must be providing you with lots of material to write about.'

The problem is that I spent a good fifty years living, working and pondering the world before I understood it well enough to scratch out a story or two. And in the blink of an eye, the world has changed.

Essentially, I see the world as a winner-take-all capitalist economy that pretends to be a civilisation. Now, don't get me wrong, I'm not a pessimist. I also see the world chock-a-block full of decent, kind, generous, hard-working, funny and creative people, who everyday punch out loving and meaningful lives.

Now, I haven't got a clue what to write about.

It takes a long time to write a book, edit it, get it accepted, and then come out to the world. I'm thinking, 'Hell's bells, what on earth will the world be like at that point in the future?'

The collection of short stories I was working on for my second book, will they be relevant any more, after the pandemic?

When people are permitted to un-isolate themselves, who knows what decisions will be made about the economy? Will it, as I fear, be a simple matter of kick-starting the beast back into action? Business as usual. Back to work, folks. Debts to be paid off, got to keep the economy growing. Or will we wake up a bit and understand that a growing economy is the problem and not the solution?

In the meantime, I'll scratch around a bit. The chooks out in the backyard have taught me a few things. Don't stop scratching, there's a juicy worm or two out there in the dirt.

Sunday, 29 March 2020

6.28 a.m.

In other news:

Climate Change Activists Reflect Upon the Good Old Days When They Could at Least Get Some Media Coverage

Indigenous Australians Put Uluru Statement From the Heart Into Time Capsule to Be Opened in 2088

Wars Rage Unabated Across the Globe – Experts Warn This Could Become a Panconflict

Mineral Exploration in National Parks Deemed an Essential Service That Must Continue

Thursday, 9 April 2020

5.46 a.m.

Let us not forget that when the pandemic is over, the LNP want to 'snap back'. Scott Morrison may well regret that choice of words. And, let us not forget that the LNP has rejected each and every amendment that the ALP has proposed to make the bailout fairer and accessible to more Australians.

Friday, 10 April 2020

4.33 a.m.

The Little Room Where I Write

It was four twenty-two when I got up this morning,

A familiar time,

Often I wake at that exact minute of the day,

And as you will note above, my electronic journal indicates it has taken me eleven minutes to get to this keyboard.

I'm in a little room, I don't know its purpose, this room. It's too small for a bedroom, too large for a closet, And it's directly off the kitchen where I make coffee in eleven minutes.

The first sip of coffee wakes up my bowel and I will head off to the bathroom, not too far away as it turns out in this house. And I'll take my ereader and read a free book, for a chapter or two, while I let go of what my body has no use for.

Sometimes when the swell is low, I fish on the rock platform near where the sewer flows out into the ocean.

I have just started reading *Notes from the Underground* by Dostoevsky. A lot has been said and written about this book. I found it for free, it is in the public domain. Some people still try to make money out of this book, you could too if you wanted. You package it up and publish it in print or ebook, and market it somehow to get sales. Imagine that, making a living out of the work of long-dead authors.

These are my morning thoughts.

When I fish off the rock platform, I wonder about the fish in the water near the outfall of human excrement. It is treated, the excrement, that is. You can smell some sort of additive, a bit like detergent.

4.56 a.m.

I'm finished in the bathroom.

When this house was built, there were no sewers. That was a long time ago, and if this house were a book, it would be in the public domain. But it wasn't free, this house, not by a long shot.People are still making money out of buildings hundreds of years old. They should attach notebooks to houses with a chain, and every owner should write some stuff in it. It should be against the law for anyone to remove or destroy or damage in any way the observations of the owners or renters who dwell in our buildings.

Maybe then I'd know more about this little room,
Too small for a bedroom,
Too big for a closet,
Where I write in the early morning with a coffee beside me.

Saturday, 11 April 2020

6.54 a.m.
Must get a bottle brush.

Sunday, 19 April 2020

6.43 a.m.
So

So, the world keeps spinning,
it hasn't slowed one iota.
Though the rumbling has subsided,
so say the seismologists.

So, consequently,
due to such spinning,
the sun still rises and yes it still sets.
She never stops moving,
either, latitudinally by the season,
or, longitudinally by the hour.

So, we get out when we can
to bathe in the reddened light,
and the digital cameras still work,
for the moment that is.

So, in the light of the day,
when totally lost in the wonder of just being,
when unrushed and unharried,
don't feel tempted to hug the nearest stranger,
lest you be called a silly so and so.

Wednesday, 29 April 2020

4.32 a.m.

Letter to my grandchildren's grandchildren.

After the opportunity presented by the Covid-19 pandemic of 2020, the very worst thing happened. The leaders of the world and their corporate billionaire overlords convinced a significant percentage of the masses that returning to normal was the only option for a brighter future. Collapse not only sped up, collapse became inevitable, unstoppable, ineluctable – insert whatever fatalistic adjective you desire.

And talk about desire, it was desire, or more precisely the fear of the end of desire, that permeated the propaganda to convince the masses to stagger back to the grindstones of consumerism. Thus sealing the fate of this latest iteration of large-scale human civilisation.

Ironically, in the early twenty-first century we were fully aware of the history of the psychopaths in charge of imperial Rome who staged more and more extravagant and violent entertainment to appease the masses while the largest civilisation ever, up to that point in time, was chaotically falling into the abyss. And yet we couldn't see how this was happening in our own massive global village.

As the collapse sped up, we distracted ourselves and congratulated ourselves.

We held Olympic games and streamed them on 5G technology to

every corner of the world, no matter what other hellish disasters played out elsewhere.

But what about those who could not ignore the facts? How did they manage to feel fine when it was the end of the world as we knew it? What did they do when collapse was inevitable? When activism was pointless? When sustainability was impossible? When growth itself was killing us?

The hopeful idealists proposed ideas: better education, holding our governments to account, new green deals, greater equality. The antsy activists proposed action: rise up, demand change, depose the tyrants, eliminate the fascists, revolution. But the machine could not be turned off.

Most people, knowing and feeling it was all too late, either consciously or not, ignored the idealists and activists and simply got on with life and enjoyed it the very best they could. They worked and raised families, made some money to spend on things and experiences that comforted their souls and contributed somehow to a sense of fulfilment. Nothing grandiose. Just day-to-day stuff.

We surrendered. We fell with grace. The globalised monetised civilisation was too far advanced and complex to save. Yes, a shame in many ways. Modern civilisation created so many things of worth, and many ideas of worth. Yet billions died, not from old age, but from famine and war and plague. Some proposed it would end with a bang, others proposed a whimper. It ended up being a series of bangs and whimpers which went on for a considerable time. So much disappeared. Buried, or reclaimed by the forests.

Let it be known to you humans of the future, that many of us could see the writing on the wall, could see that the natural way of things for the civilisation that flourished on the cheap, abundant, and dirty energy contained in our fossilised ancestors was destined to collapse in spectacular and absolute fashion.

And let it also be known that for many many decades, good people, decent people, typical humans, tried with all their intelligence and might and courage to stop the collapse. And that during the pandemic of 2020, many people in isolation, with a reprieve from the daily rat race required to prop up the utterly unsustainable, yearned for and cried out for a stop to all the madness. They called out endless growth for what it was, a childish fantasy, a denial of death, a religious pipe dream. But as history will record, after the pandemic the very worst things happened.

And finally, let it be known that though our idiotic and evil actions led some people to believe that Homo sapiens is fundamentally flawed and destined to extinction, many more people maintained a view that humans are innately good and decent beings and are capable of organising themselves in groups with systems of knowledge and governance that are sustainable. The Aboriginal peoples of the continent called Australia being the ultimate proof of that.

Take care and enjoy whatever stage your civilisation is in,

One of your great great grandparents.

This Morning's Walk

The air is full of smoke and dust and virus.

Tyson's mask is in his school bag.

Grampa let him take it off as soon as they were out of sight of home. 'Can you smell the smoke, Tiger?' he asked.

'Ye...ah,' replied the seven-year-old.

'Take it off then. It isn't working.'

Grampa has told his daughter, Tyson's mother, 'Next year, Tiger should be allowed to walk to school on his own. He'll be nine then and kids these days are being mollycoddled to their own detriment.' He has come across this information more than once. Child psychologists are writing about it on the internet and being interviewed on radio, television and podcasts. It is falling on deaf ears. Parents are too full of fear to hear rational and pertinent advice.

The street is full of large expensive four-wheel drives trying to park. The forty k sign flashes red.

Tyson and his grandfather weave their way through the frantic mothers and demanding children who clog the pathway outside the catholic school. The public school is further along the street. They pass a large electronic traffic sign that has been reprogrammed to urge residents to use water wisely.

'A hundred and fifty litres of water should be enough per person per day, eh, Gramps?'

'You'd think so.'

The rivers are empty yet two gushing streams of tears track down the dusty landscape of Grampa's face.

The Hub

Ever since everything went to shit, we meet each morning in the kitchen and on goes the kettle. We are lucky to have an old wood stove, a Canberra. Other people have to cook outdoors on makeshift barbecues. We are experimenting with local plants for the best tea. As we wander around, further and further, we are coming across more and more contenders for our daily morning beverage. Lemon myrtle is the mainstay at the moment.

We meet in the kitchen to plan our day. Food is the number one priority. We have our home garden but also a community garden that has been set up on a vacant block down the street. The couple who run that garden, good on them, are a bit too much in charge. So each of us would prefer to go fishing, or hunting, or gathering, or working in our own plot, rather than do the allocated time in the community garden. But we don't complain and we do what we have to.

The place next door is abandoned. So we move our kids and their kids in there. We take down the dividing fence. It's old hardwood and burns well.

The woman across the road, who does bugger all but whinge, and who we regularly deliver food to, despite her doing no time at all in the community garden, dutifully informs us that we cannot take over the abandoned house. 'Somebody owns it, you know,' she squawks.

We know. And we know that the owner owns dozens of properties and he lives in Sydney, which is now a difficult four-day journey away. We laugh one morning around the Canberra as we sip our teas, that if the owner turns up to kick us out, we will offer him some dried fish for rent, but only if he fixes the leak in the roof.

Fresh and dried fish have been our saviour. You could call it our primary industry. We trade it for all sorts of stuff. So when we meet in the mornings, we fire up the Canberra and talk about the tides and the swell and the wind and what possibilities exist. When the fish are on, we all go. All other activities suspended. Sometimes we even team up with another family that live across the channel. They specialise in other forms of seafood, like crabs and shellfish. They are also tuned in to the weather and the seasonal patterns. So when the whiting are running, for example, they help us out. Likewise, when needed, we will work with them for a day or two. We have a great recipe for pipis that we cook on the wood stove in our kitchen.

More and more people are leaving the area. Usually, they head south to Sydney because they have family there. Once the oil stopped coming from overseas, it was only three weeks before every car in this country became redundant. Well, that's not exactly true. Electric cars ran for an extra month until the electricity grid collapsed. One local family who owned a Nissan Leaf, which they could charge from the solar panels on their roof, managed to keep their car going for six months. They traded rides for food for a while. We had a local taxi service. But then they got a puncture, and then the spare got a puncture, and for a while people donated wheels off their redundant cars, but then a tiny part inside the electric engine went bung. That was the last car to run in this area. We have heard of a fellow further up the coast who still runs an old VW Kombi on biodiesel. But we all know that the era of the automobile is over.

No one can really say they had no idea that this was coming. We had our heads in the sand. We couldn't imagine a world without cars or electricity. Some of us remember when mobile phones didn't exist. Then when they came along, we couldn't imagine how we lived without them. But we did. And now we live without so many things that we thought were essential. On mornings around the Canberra, which we call the Hub, we sometimes remember with fondness things like Spotify and Bluetooth. Some of the newbies, born after the end of fossil fuels, have no idea what we are talking about. And it isn't easy to explain.

And though we miss some of the technologies, we have to agree that this new world, emerging from the whimpering end of the old world, has a lot going for it. Like our morning meetings at the Hub, with the smell of woodsmoke and the promise of the day ahead, fishing or gardening, or walking in the forest to find whatever it offers up. And we sing and make our own music as we work and play in our local surrounds. And on full moons we go to the Big Hub, the market park down by the channel, and eat and drink and dance with those of us who remain. Then we walk home by the light of the moon and sleep in our beds, warm and dry.

Sometimes in the morning we don't say much at all. We might already know what needs to be done on that day. Mother Nature dictates the day's events. No planning required. And when the Hub is quiet, you can hear the crackle of wood burning, birds singing, and human lips sipping on a hot cup of tea. Not a car or a plane to be heard.

Not everything went to shit.

The Principle of Almost Endless Limitations

An extract from *Musings on a Theory of Everything*, Volume I (alternatively titled *TOE Jam*), by Frank Admission

In the beginning, there was a dot, with no dimensions, not even time.

Then there was a bang, and everything began.

Up, down, left, right, forwards, backwards.

Three dimensions growing, growing in time.

Time can't exist in a dot because everything exists in one place. Time is just a consequence of the universe being in its middle phase, the phase we are in now, the space-time phase. So you can't be everywhere at once.

This is the first limitation. You can't be everywhere at once.

Time is merely separation, just like distance. And much as we want unity, strive for it, yearn for it, grieve its absence and dream of its return, it will only become a reality again at the very end, when the universe collapses and everything is once again a dot.

All suffering is the yearning for unity, for being everywhere at once, dimensionless and timeless. We get hints of this possibility every once in a while, when absorbed in a book, or lost in some all-consuming task of construction or creation. These moments are vestiges of the primal dot unity, the beginning and end points of this thing we call universe. In these rare moments, our minds become detached from time and space, and we feel peace and a oneness with all things. It's a lovely feeling. Enjoy these fleeting moments. And try – because try is all we can do – try not to wish for life to be like this at all times and in all places.

All the bits and pieces of the dot spread out through space-time are connected by the strings of light and the primal force of gravity. And light, in all its glorious wavelengths, and gravity, have a maximum speed. The quest for faster than the speed of light travel, which is a direct consequence of our desire to be everywhere at once, is futile.

This is the second limitation. You can't exceed the speed of light.

Gravity is equal and opposite to the original force that exploded the dot. And the force that exploded the dot is equal to the amount of light and matter contained in the dot and we don't know what that is. So we don't know when time will reverse and all the bits and pieces will begin to come together again. And we will never know this because we are just a bit or a piece of the dot. And a part can never fully know the whole.

This is the third limitation. You can't know everything.

But you yourself are not a single bit. You are an eddy of flotsam in the great gushing of the expansion of the exploded dot. So you can never know yourself fully. You will get hints and moments of peace and freedom and unity of self, and you can assemble a picture or a story of yourself. And you can repaint it and rewrite it and add in more detail and erase mistakes, and this can be a lifelong and rewarding hobby.

This is the fourth limitation. You can't fully know yourself.

And you are not the only human eddy of flotsam on planet earth, there are many human eddies. So you are a you that can never know itself fully, and part of a we, the population. Like all things in this stage of the universe, the expanding stage, the population has grown and expanded across the surface of the crust of the spinning earth. It is natural. And it is natural that these parts are connected by gravity and light and as humans we create connections with all sorts of stories and paintings and songs. And much as we can't stop the expansion and separation, no matter how many advances there are in the technology of transport and communication, we will never be one, much as we yearn for and dream about us all being part of one big happy family. It will never happen. Well, not in the expansion stage of the universe when the arrow of time runs in the direction of expansion. Utopia is impossible. Utopia can only exist in the dot, the dimensionless and timeless dot.

This is the fifth limitation. You can't create a perfect world.

The limitations go on and on. No person will ever know every limitation. It appears that the number of limitations is endless. This is no surprise, because we are such tiny bits of the dot. But the dot is everything and everything has a beginning, middle and end, and thus is finite. Infinity is an idea and not a reality. There is a finite number of limitations; call this a limitation itself if you are so philosophically inclined. But for our tiny minds, with our own limited time as an eddy of organic flotsam on the finite eddy of planet earth, there is an almost endless number of limitations. We will only get to know a relatively small number of them.

Now, here is the good news. In between each limitation, there is an almost endless number of possibilities. This is where we can dwell, this is where we can experience moments of peace and unity with every other entity that originated from the dot. And only when we understand that there exists an almost endless number of limitations, and thus an almost endless number of possibilities, can we be content with all that we do have.

Longing

In his head is a longing. Is it for home, whatever that may be? Is it a longing to discover the ultimate truth about things? He doesn't know. All he knows is he is wandering aimlessly around the temperate and subtropical zones of a nation continent that is itself lost.

There are no connections to country that run deeper than the present feelings and ideas he has about the landscape he finds himself in. No connection to country.

There are no ancestral roots other than the memories of a wrecked nuclear family. No ancestral roots.

There are no goals other than to pay for rent and food and whatever needs present themselves, daily, weekly, monthly. He lives in the confused present. No goals.

No country, no roots, no goals, only longing.

Have a go, they say. He's been having a go for as long as he can recall. Has it given him wealth, or peace, or meaning? No.

What is wealth? Is it personal or common? He doesn't sense a hint of any of it. He is not dirt poor. There are cypress floorboards under his feet. Scratched and worn from a hundred pairs of disconnected feet. The negatively geared landlord's boards. He recalls the lino floors, slate floors and threadbare stained carpet floors that he has parked on sporadically for leased periods. None that he could call his own. Other people's floors. Other people's flaws. He is clothed, other people's clothes, there are tons of them every week, new second-hand stock available from dozens of local charity outlets. Other people's chuck outs, some hardly worn. He is fed. New specials at the supermarket every week. Not dirt poor, not naked poor, not starving poor. Poor in some other way, a way he can't grasp, let alone speak.

The kerbs are guttered and people tend to their nature strips. Behind the fences are sounds of children playing and the smell of onions frying. The lucky country. The land of a fair go for those who have a go. He is finding it harder and harder to have a go. The common wealth is slipping away. Reality, broadcast daily, episode after episode, season after season, real people cooking real food and renovating real homes. Reality in your face, yet slipping away.

He gets an idea. I am longing for reality, whatever that is. Go for a walk and see what I can find.

Some people utter g'days, some just nod, and then there are those who smile. The smiles are best, a touch of belonging to a species of decent social beings who care for each other. A simple movement of the mouth to engender warmth and solidarity. There is hope, despite the calamitous weather, and the spawning of viral mutations, and the eruptions of chaotic mass rage. Despite the ever present sense that the whole shebang is ending. Bang, whimper, bang, whimper.

Some people just pass by. No acknowledgement, they walk, or run, or cycle. Not even a nod or a ding of their bicycle bell on the shared pathway. They're in their own heads, Bluetooth buds blocking out the neighbourhood. Regardless, the sun rises. A word pops into his head – prosper. With no dictionary at hand, he composes his own definition. Prosper, verb, to live without longing. Prosperity, noun, the state of living without longing.

Prosperity? A goal, perhaps? Prosperity for self or for nation? For both, of course. But how? With no home, no family and bugger all understanding of how it all works, he walks on, familiar with this place where his head and heart find themselves, today.

The shared pathway loops back to where he began, longing just a little bit less than before.

June–July 2020

Sunday, 14 June 2020

5.58 a.m.

Looking ahead not getting ahead.

It's raining again. A hundred per cent humidity in winter. Mobile phones warn of moisture detected. It's hard to recall the feeling of that last hot dry summer. The royal commission into the bushfires publishes testimonies of unimaginable horror and analyses of inadequate preparations and responses, yet I can't fully remember or reimagine what it was like back then. There is the present to deal with – a new set of dramas unfolding. Disease and the economy. Systemic racism being exposed in our institutions. Not even our beloved artists are exempt from this new revision of history and culture. People are massing. Lip service from politicians representing governments that fail to enact the recommendations of repeated inquiries will no longer suffice. Do something, we scream. People now demanding change. Covid-19 a trigger point. The real issues have nothing to do with a biological virus and everything to do with social justice. If the world is not ending just yet, it feels that the era of unfettered individualism has run its course. The 'human race', that ridiculous scramble to 'get ahead', is over. Who do we want to get ahead of? Our brothers and sisters? The other team? Some other state or nation? There is no fundamental right to 'get ahead'. We survive and thrive as a society, not as billions of individuals racing against each other. The fires and the droughts and the relentless ocean and the mutating viruses remind us that money and fame, titles and degrees, and beauty and personal health, mean nothing when Mother Nature settles the score.

Saturday, 11 July 2020

6.55 a.m.

Lost.

So much information and knowledge and wisdom have been lost from past civilisations. And what will be lost forever when the current modern civilisation that you and I find ourselves in gets buried under the sands of time? What will our children's, children's children wonder about the past which is our present? Will these descendants be able to access electronically recorded sound and video? Will books and art recorded in a hard physical form be the only truly accessible links to the past? Though, it's not unthinkable that a vinyl disc, etched with the vibrations of the past, could be easily deciphered. Perhaps even magnetic tape with its analog waves of information might be relatively simple to decode. But what about the stockpile of digital information stored on hard drives and computer chips? Could they remain forever mysterious artefacts of the past, undecipherable, the key to their unlocking beyond the reach of our descendants who arise from the ruins of the modern world?

Tuesday, 28 July 2020

5.37 a.m.

Distractions

In the morning, he thinks he has to have coffee,

So he has coffee.

And then he thinks he needs to go to the gym,

So he goes to the gym.

On the way he listens to the radio and hears a politician not answering any of the questions being asked.

He gets cranky and for a moment forgets he is going to the gym.

He remembers just in time and turns off at the correct intersection.

He wonders if the girl he fancies will be there.

She's a good distraction.

Later, someone at work asks if he watched the final on television last night.

He gives his opinion, and the question asker gives their opinion. Mindless office chit-chat, a welcome distraction.

At the staff meeting scheduled just after lunch, a new policy is unveiled.

The jargon is so absurd that he laughs. A silent and expressionless laugh. Work: an endless series of policies and accountabilities documented and replicated in emails and hard copy printed on dead trees and filed into filing cabinets that fill faster than they can be emptied into archive boxes that end up in a storage facility located in an industrial area on the outskirts of an expanding suburban region on the outskirts of an expanding metropolis on an ever shrinking planet.

Someone exhales, thank God it's Friday. Plans are made for drinks and eats. The week has to be dissolved.

The world is full of distractions, thankfully, he thinks. The thought of an unobstructed view of reality is too frightening to contemplate.

The Map

She packed the obligatory spare pair of undies. And she packed the map. She could have probably left the map behind because its contours and legend were practically tattooed on her body. She could have consulted the map whenever she looked at herself in the mirror, a habit she acquired early on by aping her mother and older sisters.

To be safe, and you have to always be safe, she folded the map carefully and placed it in the backpack along with the undies and the make-up essentials she had been trained to use since the age of ten. She could hear her mother: 'Don't forget the undies, and don't you even think of walking out the front door without your face done.'

She was sixteen, and though the map clearly illustrated the world as a dangerous place filled with sex-hungry-no-hoper-conmen, she just knew somehow, her gut was telling her, she had to get out, get away, get some air.

She took a face mask as well. The secret one she kept. A secret because her mother and sisters laughed at the people they called sheeple who donned masks and washed their hands. The idiots who blindly obeyed the government that was controlled by the alien lizard people who owned Big Pharma.

It was still dark when she slid out through her bedroom window. The mother and the sisters would be getting their beauty sleep. Beauty was important and not to be let wither and die. Her father slept out on the front porch, not becoming more beautiful, but sleeping off the beer and whisky he drank out of necessity, as he put it. She sneaked around to the back of the house to avoid the father and any early-bird gentlemen callers who might be parked in the street. The sisters were undoubtedly the best catches in town. There might even be a group of boys on bicycles waiting in the street to see her, the youngest, sweet sixteen and never been kissed, by anyone other than her father, that was.

The map depicted the town in which the young girl lived as an island. It was connected to the rest of the world by bridges that disappeared off the edges of the map. When she dared ask questions about the other worlds out there, she was dutifully informed that the map covered everywhere and everything that was important.

'Silly girl! The map is a perfect representation of the world as it is. It was drawn by the greatest cartographer in the world. You know, Mr Wainwright?'

'Oh, him.'

She'd heard many times how Mr Wainwright fancied her mother. It was worth boasting about as he was the richest and most famous man in town. He mixed with all the celebrities and held the most wonderful parties. Apparently, though, and this was why Mother always rejected his advances, he had a small penis. Pinky size. Whenever penis size was brought up in family conversation, which was often, Mr Wainwright would be mentioned and Mother and the sisters would laugh and raise their pinkies, while Father would nod and rub his belly with self satisfaction, as he, and all the girls knew it, was well hung.

She couldn't jump over the back fence quick enough.

After years of trying and failing to find a better life, to find her tribe, to find her place on the planet, to find the perfect lover, to find peace and happiness, she began to consider returning home. At least there, her map of the world would make sense. Even if that world was constructed of pain and fear and stitched together with lies and unfounded braggadocio.

Then she met the counsellor. She was dragged there by her flatmate. Dragged to the government-funded service to help women like her – women who were fatally attracted to abusive men. Broken women. Women with scars and bruises mapped all over their skin.

In the first session, the counsellor listened. She heard the story of a girl who ran away at sixteen from an incestuous family only to stumble repetitively through life. An endless succession of falling in with the wrong people, both men and women. Men and women who she trusted and strove to please. People who invariably ended up cheating and lying and stealing from her. People who charmed and flattered her at first only to turn on her like junkyard dogs. The counsellor also heard about the decent people who for some unfathomable reason she would always end up letting down and consequently losing from her life.

Having heard this story many times before, the counsellor didn't really need to make notes, but did so as required by the regulatory body.

'What are you writing?' she asked at one point with fear in her eyes.

The counsellor spoke calmly and honestly about the purpose and requirements of the notes.

'Will anyone be able to come here and demand to see these notes?'

'Not even a policeman or a court judge will be able to demand to see what I have written. The privacy of our meetings is sacrosanct.'

Though she didn't know the meaning of sacrosanct, she felt at ease with the counsellor. She could hear something, or was there something she didn't hear, in the tone of their voice. She'd experienced this before with the decent people she'd come across occasionally in her life on the run. It was unsettling at first, hearing people speak quietly and calmly and with no great theatrics. She was suspicious of these people. She couldn't find a symbol for them on her map. And though she felt they were perhaps the right people she should be associating with, she would somehow manage to always fuck things up and either they would go away, or more likely, she would go away with a familiar nauseating cocktail of guilt and confusion sloshing around in her stomach.

In each of the following sessions, the counsellor would consult their notes and draw upon some section of the story recounted in session one. Then would come questions: 'And what they said to you, was that true?'; 'Why do you think you believed it?'; 'How do you feel when you are recalling these events from the past?'

Invariably, she would be unable to answer these questions about truth and belief and feelings, and she would end up in tears, sometimes howling like an injured animal.

The counsellor would smile at the end of each session and say that she was doing well. 'You are making progress. It is going to take some time, but you will get through this. I know because I have seen so many women like you come to understand what they have been through and then be able to begin the process of healing. You are stronger than you think, and the truth is being told, here and now. You will slowly begin to discover that you are worthy of love, especially your own love.'

After each session, she felt a strange lightness. And yet, before each new session, she felt an enormous weight. A weight that threatened to stop her going. A weight she couldn't explain to her flatmate, who would drag her by the hand to the next session.

'Remember the lightness you feel after each session? Get in there. I'll be here, waiting.'

And she would go. She was determined not to lose yet another decent friend. And as before, she would experience confusion and cry and howl, and discover the truth of her suffering. She had wished for peace and freedom; she never imagined it would come like this.

At session six, the counsellor explained that they could write a report to the agency and gain more funding. 'Six more?'

She nodded.

'Good on you,' said the counsellor. 'But before you come back, there is something I want you to do.'

She twitched. It was a tic of sorts that was triggered whenever someone asked her to do something.

The counsellor noticed the discomfort, 'Only do it if you want to.'

'What is it?' she asked.

'The map. I assume you still have it?'

'Yes, I do.'

'Burn it.'

Returns and Resignations

The clouds were threatening, rumbling and roiling for days. And it was humid. If only the clouds would burst and rain and refresh the air. It was only October. 'Unseasonal,' people said.

In bed, on their phones, Marsha checked the stock market and James checked the Bureau of Meteorology.

'Any rain coming?' asked Marsha.

'None on the radar. Let me check the forecast.' James tapped the screen, waited, then tapped again.

Marsha put her phone onto the bedside table and waited. James could feel her eyes upon him. A familiar tension built in his shoulders. She was an impatient one, Marsha.

'Well? Is it going to rain? We should wash these sheets, you know. They smell like man.'

'Hang on. I keep pressing the wrong link.'

'Forget it.' Marsha flung the sheets aside and without another word, or look, left the matrimonial bed and left the room.

All the recent talk about loneliness in an overpopulated world was true. James felt it not only in his shoulders, but in his gut, and strangely, in his left elbow, an electric twang whenever Marsha shunned him. She would be in the spare room now, dressing for the gym. James knew her routine well. He will then hear her grabbing the car keys off the hook and she will call out, 'I'm off,' and then add in some chore for him to complete while she worked on defying the ageing process. He wagered to himself that this morning she will want him to wash the man-smelling sheets.

What's wrong with male odour, thought James as he read no rain for the rest of the week. What's wrong with Marsha? What's wrong with me? Why am I here? Suffering a loveless, lonely life? I have waited so long for her to change. People change, don't they? I am weak, he admitted to himself.

'I'm off,' she called. 'If it isn't going to rain, can you wash the sheets, please?'

Reads like a reasonable request, doesn't it? But it was not. If you heard the tone, you would understand. The two-syllable *please*, in particular, said it all. But it was only James who heard this Marsha. Everyone else heard another Marsha, the public Marsha, the Marsha who James fell in love with and married. Married in a church of all places. James occasionally fantasised that his marriage must be null and void. His atheism, unshakeable and formed long before he met Marsha, surely negated his declaration of till death do us part, made in the presence of God. But he did sign the certificate.

Marsha's desire to marry was expressed early, in the days of limerence. Blinded by brain chemicals, James would do anything for Marsha. He even willingly acted out the role she created for him in her idealised marriage proposal scenario. After he got down on his knee and declared his undying love, and presented the ring she had already chosen, in front of the whole dinner party she had organised for her own birthday, he didn't feel anything of a sucker. Now, James gets that electric twang in the elbow whenever he recalls that night. Blinded.

The sheets, the most expensive flax linen, clumped in the spin cycle and bumped the washing machine out of action. Beep, beep…rebalance me, please. Even the machines were bossing poor James around. James, the kept man. Being a house dad was great when the kids were around. Cooking and craft, camping and fishing, caring and loving, reciprocated loving, the kids unconditional in every way.

When the youngest, Lydia, finished year 12, James proposed looking for a job. 'I wouldn't mind getting back into the department. Be nice to have some adult social interaction.'

'No,' Marsha responded. 'I need you here. We don't need the money, and you can thank my father for that. Be grateful. Not many men your age don't have to work.'

'I need to get out of this house.'

'It's not all about you, James. Be grateful for God's sake.'

When she said his name, James, with the rising inflection, he knew to give up.

With the kids gone, he took up gardening. He made a friend at the plant nursery, Ken with the mullet hairdo. James would show Ken photos of the backyard, or the difficult side yards, and the nursery man never failed with his plant suggestions. The mango tree in the sunny back corner was thriving, even this far south of the tropics.

'You don't want rain when it's flowering, though,' said Ken.

James looked at the sky as he hung out the sheets. It's almost green, he thought. And it's rumbling, again. The mango flowers were out, a promise of late summer fruit. Stay away, rain. I need something to look forward to.

Inside, James put new sheets onto the bed. It was unlikely with this humidity and no wind that the sheets on the line would dry in time. Marsha didn't make beds. Marsha paid the bills. To be accurate, the dividends on her inherited share portfolio paid the bills, and then some. Marsha bought James a fancy red Fiat when he succumbed and agreed not to go back to work. He didn't want a new car, especially a red one, but she was paying and who was he to complain? And she paid for the business class airfares whenever they travelled interstate or overseas to visit the kids. Marsha hoped the travel bans would be lifted soon. James didn't. He thought their kids deserved the freedom they had obviously sought when they distanced themselves so dramatically from the family.

He missed the kids terribly, but he was happy to let them go. He was maybe even a bit jealous that they could so easily up and leave.

The house was quiet. The fridge struggled in the humidity and the motor kicked in as he opened the freezer door. He remembered, 'Lamb back straps for dinner, please.' Only the best cuts of meat for Marsha. She was a meat eater, that's for sure. 'And now *everyone's* into keto,' she boasted. 'I was ahead of my time.' James was meat, he knew that much.

But he reckoned he was devon in Marsha's eyes. Processed lips and arse, supposedly. James, processed beyond redemption.

Marsha was flirting with the Covid marshal at the gym when the news first broke. She'd done her warm-up run on the treadmill and was lined up on the taped crosses on the carpeted floor for the barre attack class. Troy, the marshal, would have been twenty years her junior, but Marsha had felt his eyes, and the not so subtle positioning of his hands as he assisted with her alignment in pilates. Not that Marsha would ever have an affair. She just liked the attention, the acknowledgement that she had beaten the weathering effects of time. She liked the power. And like all narcissists, deep down she was insecure and fearful. Fearful to the extent that she needed to control the world. An affair, with its nakedness and potential for chaos, was way too scary for Marsha.

The gym was full of television screens but not one was tuned into the news. There was music, sports, fashion and clean-food channels only. Motivational. Inspirational. The stock market collapse was going on outside, the gym junkies oblivious.

James had ABC radio on as he marinated the back straps. The shock and surprise in the announcers' voices was something he hadn't heard since 9/11. He switched on the television and saw real horror on the faces of the talking heads. Sure, the GFC in 2008 caused the same sort concern and seriousness of discussion. But this was not a correction, this was collapse. Banks were closing their doors. It would only be a matter of time before suits started jumping from tall buildings.

Marsha first heard the news at the hairdressers after gym. Immediately, she rang James. His phone was on the kitchen bench, streaming ABC. James was out the back, hanging out the sheets and checking the mango flowers and the threatening skies. Hold off, rain, he prayed to the God he didn't believe in. Marsha cursed when her call went to voicemail. Then she noticed he had texted.

Some problems at the stock market. Maybe contact the broker.

She cursed again. She'd already heard from the girls at the saloon that sixty per cent had been wiped off in the first hour and that a ninety per cent fall, like the collapse of '29, was expected.

'He should have rung the broker,' she screamed out aloud.

All heads turned towards Marsha. She ran out into the car park and collapsed next to her BMW.

The back straps remained marinated and uncooked that day. Marsha berated James for not doing more to save her wealth. He didn't bother pointing out that it was actually their wealth. That as her husband, her stay-at-home-and-raise-the-kids husband, that by marriage vow, and God, and by the law itself, they were partners in every sense. Marsha's father died after they were married. He didn't say a thing. Years of putting up and shutting up, years of bowing to Marsha, years of succumbing to something he could never change. He let her rant and rave, accuse and blame, belittle and humiliate. It was water off a duck's back. He turned off the preheated stove and retrieved a beer from the struggling fridge. He didn't offer Marsha a wine – there was no empty space in her tirade to insert an invitation.

Initially, James had never felt better. He noted an obvious absence of any sharp twanging in the left elbow. Something had shifted in him, and in her. He became aware that Marsha's power and dominance were evaporating. Quite ironic, he thought, since nothing else was evaporating in all this humidity.

In the days and weeks that followed, the world changed. The stock market was wiped out. Real estate values plummeted. The pandemic became yesterday's news. For a while, death from Covid seemed, for many, like a desirable outcome.

The rain did come eventually. It washed the air and there was a sense of hope, if you were open to it. People began sharing and caring for each other. James looked forward to a bumper crop from his mango tree which he would share with his neighbours. The rain had held off long enough for the fruit to set.

One day, down the track, when so much had been lost financially, and yet so much gained in every other measure of human existence, in a last-ditch pathetic attempt to regain some control, Marsha told James, 'I want you to leave. Pack your stuff and get out.'

'I need to stay home, you told me that yourself when I wanted to get back into the workforce. What's changed?'

Marsha threw the pair of scissors she had in her hand at James. He ducked, she missed. She came at him with arms flailing. She was frothing at the mouth. Red in the face. He grabbed her in a hug, her arms useless at close range. She began to cry. He held her tight. He let her sob. He led her to the bedroom.

'Lie down. I changed the sheets today,' he said as calm as calm. 'Have a rest, I'll cook some dinner.'

'Fuck off,' she sobbed in a resigned tone.

James left the room smiling. Maybe now she will soften and change back to the person I married, he thought.

He browned the gravy beef and cut up some potatoes he had dug up earlier from the vegie patch out the back.

August–September 2020

Tuesday, 4 August 2020

5.32 a.m.

Curiosity may have killed the cat, but for humans, curiosity is the stuff of life. Those who question and search for knowledge do not tire, they do not succumb to mediocrity or submit to convention, they do not subscribe to dogmatic religion or conspiracy theories. They do not become slaves to whatever system of economics is prevailing at the time. They live full and rewarding lives regardless of whether the civilisation in which they find themselves is rising or falling, or at war with itself, or in a period of peace.

Wednesday, 19 August 2020

6.36 a.m.

This is the lie the neoliberals want us to believe:

Schools and workplaces must remain open for the well-being of all. Schools and workplaces are essential for the economy. A healthy economy, such as the one we had before the pandemic, is good for everyone. Humans who can't attend school or work will suffer mental health problems. Without school, children will become lazy, undisciplined and dumb. Without jobs, adults will become lazy, unproductive and dependent on government welfare.

Here are some truths:

Schools and universities have been slowly but surely evolving into training institutions to produce workers that are useful for the economy. Workplaces have slowly but surely been de-unionised for the sole purpose of profit which is not shared with the workers. The economy we had before the pandemic gushed money to the top, the trickle down only kept workers one or two paydays away from defaulting on mortgage payments to the banks or rent payments to landlords. The fear of losing the roof over your head is the main cause of mental health issues arising from lockdowns. Children are naturally curious learning machines, and for aeons, long before the invention of 'the economy', humans have cooperatively worked together to efficiently and creatively meet their needs and wants and solve the problems of surviving and thriving.

Don't be fooled by the propaganda.

Saturday, 19 September 2020

5.50 a.m.

The world ended.

It was only ever a matter of time.

People denied it, fought it, got drunk, fornicated and looted. It was unstoppable. It wasn't one thing, but a host of things, a host of things all coming together with an ineluctable synergy. You name it, it happened. Mass extinction, yep, it happened. War, that happened too. So did plague, pestilence, ecological collapse, economic collapse, climate change, famine and violent revolution. To be accurate, though, there was no asteroid impact or alien invasion.

A perfect storm said the reporters before reporting ended. It didn't happen quickly, like a bang, but it spluttered to the finish line. And there was lots of whimpering. That poet was right.

Infinity is a myth. So is eternity.

The world didn't really end. What ended was just the latest human civilisation. The one with aeroplanes and the internet. The one powered by fossil fuels and money. The one that extended across every continent and then dreamed it would expand into space. Mind you, Mars was looking pretty peaceful, and sunny.

Humans survived. Little isolated groups dotted here and there around the planet managed to escape the calamity of a dying civilisation. Some of these little dots were intentional dots which were created by people who called themselves Preppers, while others called them nutters. They found the remotest little corners of their environments and completely detached and isolated themselves. Other dots survived by sheer luck. Like the people who found themselves on brand-new islands formed by the rising oceans. Little life rafts for Homo sapiens.

Monday, 28 September 2020

6.15 a.m.

Prediction: The chaos in the US will continue to escalate and there is every possibility that things could get out of hand very quickly during and after the election in five weeks time.

Covid-19 was an opportunity to reset/retreat/reconcile/reconsider. It is clearly not happening. The *zeitgeist* is recovery – recover to business as usual. Stupid, stupid humans. The leaders and the followers.

The rat race has failed.

And we are living through it now.

The world is whimpering. Listen, can you hear it?

How I Became the Nostradamus of Los Angeles

I'll never forget the day back in 1991 when the police bought Vinnie into the Tank. He claimed to be a scientist, and that he came from the future, 2021 to be precise. Now, I've dealt with a lot of nut jobs in my time and you wouldn't believe some of the tall tales I've heard, but Vinnie with his story of time travel by Segway – whatever on Earth that is – the day after he married a porn star, took the cake, albeit a fruit cake.

He was christened Vinnie because he was picked up on South Vine Sreet, down at Anaheim, and there was no way that Ratched, our crotchety old triage nurse, was going to record Baron Aleku Valvazor on the intake form.

Vinnie was clearly delusional and highly agitated. 'I have to find the Segway, the Segway,' he kept ranting, along with, 'I must get back to Lissa, to Lissa, my sex god, Lissa.'

The fifty milligrams of risperidone I injected into his deltoid settled him down enough for us to get him into a straitjacket and inside the padded cell. All standard procedure. One particularly odd thing I noticed back on that very first day was how Vinnie looked like no other person I had ever seen before, or since. It's hard to describe, but the word translucent comes to mind. Or, as one of my colleagues asked me, after we had Vinnie stabilised and into his own room minus the straitjacket, 'Does Vinnie look out of focus to you?'

Over the following months, Vinnie settled into the routine here at Napa State Hospital. As one of his primary care nurses, I was privy to his psych reports. They were interesting reading. The fact that no clear diagnosis could be made was nothing new here at Napa, but in the case of Vinnie, the five psychiatrists who had examined him all had widely differing opinions on his condition.

One psych was sure that Vinnie had a dissociative disorder, but couldn't settle on which: dissociative identity disorder, depersonalization/derealisation disorder, or dissociative amnesia. The amnesia conclusion made sense since Vinnie did have difficulty providing much detail about his time at the University of Cambridge and also exactly what happened to his great uncle, Benedik, the vampire. Crazy, eh?

Another psych confidently placed Vinnie into the realm of personality disorders. Though she couldn't neatly pigeonhole him into any specific disorder. In fact, she couldn't even definitively place him into cluster A, B or C. Her best conclusion that he was a unique, perhaps one-of-a-kind, mosaic of schizotypal, narcissistic, and obsessive-compulsive personality disorders. He definitely had a high opinion of himself.

The third psych sent Vinnie's way was confident that schizophrenia was playing havoc with our man from the future's mind. Again, a clear diagnosis was not made. The notes suggest that Vinnie suffered from an exotic cocktail of paranoid schizophrenia, schizoaffective disorder and disorganised schizophrenia. Yes, this psych actually used the term 'exotic cocktail'. It was rumoured that Dr Abrahams liked a drink or six, and I had on occasion whiffed his hangover halitosis, but his observations were spot on. Vinnie would post notes on the walls of his room. One wall was full of scientific formulae, another wall was plastered with sketches of nude women, the third wall consisted of vampire poetry, and the fourth wall around the doorway was chock-a-block full of predictions of the future, such as how Bill Clinton would be elected as POTUS and be impeached for receiving, and later lying about, fellatio from a curvy, brunette intern. Though, with hindsight, I question if that was disorganised or organised. It was certainly out there.

Pysch number four went down the autism path. Again, their observations systematically matched to the DSM diagnostic criteria made sense. Again the psych couldn't be definitive. She couldn't pinpoint exactly where he sat on the spectrum and even suggested he might be a slider, the term she used for those patients who move between Asperger's, Kanner's and Rett syndromes. The day this psych visited Vinnie, he was in one of his moods which verged on catatonia. He wouldn't speak, he was hypersensitive to light and his gait was Monty Pythonesque.

Vinnie was a mystery. And though he was never violent, it was decided that he ticked enough boxes to be permanently involuntarily incarcerated. It was also decided that one more assessment was required.

The fifth psychiatrist to visit couldn't get past Vinnie's strange appearance, which incidentally, I and others had somehow grown used to. I was present during this assessment and Dr Finbar Murphy must have taken his glasses off at least dozen times. He would wipe them on his cardigan and hold them up to the fluorescent light to ensure they were clean. He would then place them back on his ruddy face and look once again at Vinnie. He even took Vinnie's arm and declared out loud that he was certain he could see the radius and ulna bones through the patient's skin and muscle.

Finbar, who us nurses liked best of all, ceased the pysch evaluation and ordered a full medical examination. 'I think you might have a nutritional deficiency, Vinnie.'

Vinnie laughed and said that his transparency was due to only being half a full human, and that his other half was in 2021, probably at this very moment performing cunnilingus on his beloved wife, Lissa Mammalia.

'Okaaay,' said Finbar. 'I'll get the results first, and then we can take it from there.'

It's totally unprofessional but absolutely necessary for us mental health nurses at NAPA to talk about the patients in our care. Outside in the staff courtyard, where we smoke – and we all smoke – we not only talked about our patients, we laughed, and we cried, and often vented anger and frustration at the system in which we found ourselves employed. I personally found Vinnie intriguing and was never bothered by his eccentricities. Denise, on the other hand, who was not known for subtlety, God bless her, labelled Vinnie a sicko pervert and refused to be alone with him at any time. I must admit, Vinnie never masturbated in my presence. I wasn't sure whether to take that personally or not. In the end, and I told the others one day after lunch out in the courtyard, how I figured that Denise's large breasts and ample buttocks, as compared to my flat chest and pancake arse, were, thankfully, the reason why I was spared from ever witnessing Vinnie batting off. We laughed and coughed smoke. And went back to work refreshed and ready to confront the lunatics for the afternoon.

The results of Vinnie's full medical, ordered by Finbar, came back negative. No underlying conditions. Though the radiologist did make note that he had to turn down the X-ray machine to fifty per cent intensity so as to get an image of Vinnie's insides. Apparently, at a hundred per cent, the X-rays went straight through Vinnie and left an almost blank image. It was odd.

Vinnie was odd. And nothing could prepare me for what was to come next.

It was a sunny winter morning when I took Vinnie out for a walk. I remember it well. The weather reflected the mood of the nation which had just voted in Bill Clinton for president. Vinnie reminded me of his prediction, which I didn't take too seriously as anyone could have predicted that outcome, and I told him so.

'Just you wait,' said Vinnie. 'Remember the name Monica, and remember it will all come unstuck with come. Come on a blue dress!'

'OK, that's enough of that talk,' I said. And either my physical unattractiveness to this odd bod, which I regarded as my Vinnie-the-wanker safety barrier, or the fact that I never took any rubbish from patients, caused him to cease in his usual tendency to spiral wildly into diatribes of ever increasing filth and depravity.

We were able to continue our walk through the lovely gum trees. I had learnt from Nathan, the groundsman, how these trees were native to Australia, the land down under with kangaroos and boomerangs which I one day hoped to visit. Vinnie asked if we could go into a clearing in a copse of these trees, and having no fear of the man, I agreed.

To my surprise, and to Vinnie's ecstatic delight, in the middle of this clearing stood a strange device that consisted of two wheels attached to the sides of a low-standing platform, from which stemmed a slender post upon which a set of handlebars were attached.

'At last,' said Vinnie. He rushed over to this odd machine and, holding onto the handles, stepped up onto the platform and said, 'It is time for me to depart, my dear. Fear not, all will be well. Thank you for your kind attention to my basic needs. I bid you farewell, and pass on my warm regards to Denise, what an arse!' With that, the strange two-wheeled transporter hummed into life and, with Vinnie aboard, sped off into the distance.

Later, when I pieced it all together, I realised that Vinni had found his so-called Segway.

Vinnie was never found. I lied and said he had run off. I was suspended while a full investigation was carried out but was cleared of any wrongdoing and tasked with clearing out his room. I took down all the bits of paper he had stuck up on the walls, and though I was meant to take them to the incinerator, I secretly stashed them into my bag and took them home, where I placed them in safe keeping. I then proceeded to forget all about them.

On 26 January 1998, nearly seven whole years after Vinnie vanished on that crazy two- wheeled machine, I watched President Clinton deny having sexual relations with an intern named Monica Lewinski. I brushed it off as a coincidence, but later that same year when the DNA on the semen-stained blue dress was matched to Bill Clinton, I had a bit of a nervous breakdown and hit the bourbon real hard. Consequently, I lost my job at Napa State Hospital.

Things were looking pretty grim until I remembered that I had all of Vinnie's predictions for the future stashed in my basement. I checked over all of his predictions dating up to the present – that is, 1992 to-1998 – and they were spot on. From Nelson Mandela becoming president of South Africa to the separation of Czechoslovakia into the Czech Republic and Slovakia. From the divorce of Princess Diana and Prince

Charles to the creation of the internet search engine Ask Jeeves. He even predicted that a fictional character named Harry Potter would arrive on the scene and hold both young and old readers in a spell. There were reams of the stuff, and most of it was still to come. I was sitting on a gold mine.

I know that this means that Vinnie must have been right all along and did actually come from the future. And if I think about it too much, I find myself once again reaching for the bottle. So I don't think about it, I just remain focused on the many ways I can monetise what I have in my possession before I retire in 2020, or thereabouts.

The rest of my future is history, sort of.

October–November 2020

Monday, 5 October 2020

5.15 a.m. AEDT (formerly 4.15 a.m. AEST)
The clock on the fridge still displays non-daylight saving time – that is, one hour earlier than all our mobile phones and computers are saying. They automatically adjust – algorithms. The clock on the fridge requires the pressing of two buttons simultaneously. Thus it stays, for the moment, on 'old time'. My watch, which requires several button presses in a unique combination I always forget, was never changed when daylight saving finished back in April, last autumn. Now it reads the correct time again.

What is the real time? Let's just say very early morning, the dark variety. Writing time.

Labour Day? A public holiday to commemorate the achievements of the union movement? A day to remember the sacrifices of workers? I'm not sure. I could Google it, but I don't like internetting early in the morning. It takes me away from writing and, before I know it, it is not early morning any more and I have become distracted and agitated from reading the opinions of the world. I lose my creative writing mojo.

Mojo? Sitting next to me on a stool is a big Australian English dictionary. I look up 'mojo'. It is colloquial for life force. It is also a word from 'US Black English' for a magic charm, amulet. I think of Black America, and I wonder if the POTUS has died overnight from Covid-19. I could look it up on the internet, but refrain. I want to write.

Specifically, I want to write my next book, which stupidly I have somehow got into my head should be a novel. Stupidly, I say, because I now have this massive thing swirling around in my head. Let's call it 'my yet to be written novel'. It's massive and morphing. I have made several starts; none have been sufficiently captivating to captivate me sufficiently. And so this thing, 'my yet to be written novel', loiters in my head and stirs up those monkey voices that tell me I am not capable of writing a novel and not sufficiently hard-working or disciplined for the task.

Novel? 'A fictitious prose narrative of considerable length' (dictionary on stool, 2020). See what I do in my allocated time for writing my next book? Stuff like this. Slack, eh?

It's OK. I like to think that I don't have unrealistic expectations of others and I try to apply the same to my self. Dropping the word 'should' from the self-talk vocabulary is a good start. Of course I'm going to struggle to get a novel under way. Of course I will struggle with keeping up the enthusiasm needed to pump out 50,000-plus words (considerable length). Of course I will question at every step of writing a novel whether this 'thing' is of any worth and, worst of all, if I am of any worth. It's OK. I'm getting better at shutting out the monkey voices.

The beginning of daylight saving, though occurring in spring, is in many ways the start of summer. I'm grateful I don't have to do physical labour in summer. Especially since summer is of considerable length – and lengthening. I'm grateful for being able to write, and for the moments of mojo experienced as I struggle with my next book (novel?), in the dark, now twilight, of early morning.

Friday, 6 November 2020

4.25 a.m.
214:264

Too close to call.

While the world waits for who will get the 270 electoral college votes needed to be president, life goes on and the media needs to report stuff. Stuff for us to consume. We hunger for it. It's nibblies at the moment while we wait for the result of this 'unprecedented' and 'most important election of all time'. The main meal is coming.

There is a lot of wondering. Wondering if the incumbent will leave the White House even if he loses fair and square as decided by the courts. Wondering if he will sign pardons for himself and others between now and January 2021. Wondering what the hell is in store for the US and the world in 2021. Wondering, even if the Democrat candidate takes the seat, how on Earth does America overcome the ugly red–blue polarisation that looks neatly geographical on the election outcome maps shown on TV but, as we know, is actually an untidy divide that exists between people who live on the same streets and even in the same families? It's not geopolitical, it's personal. The un-united states.

Is the main meal civil war?

Monday, 9 November 2020

5.55 a.m.

214:290

Biden defeats Trump. How nice was it to be a part of the collective human sigh of relief that took place yesterday?

Wednesday, 11 November 2020

4.51 a.m.

Journalist: What are your thoughts on X?

Politician: Well, let me say this, X is an important issue and I think there needs to be debate about it.

Journo: But what are your thoughts? Are you for X or against it?

Polly: It is a complex issue and we take this matter seriously, and that is why I encourage the whole of the nation to engage and to participate in the dialogue.

Journo: How about starting the dialogue now and stating your beliefs on this matter?

Polly: OK, well, we here in government…

Journo: Hang on, the government has been kicking X down the road for the last seven years. What is your position on the matter?

Polly: My position is the government's position.

Journo: But your government doesn't have a position.

Polly: Yes, we do. We are actively engaged in our communities and having that dialogue.

Journo: But that's not a position.

Polly: Well, in a democracy all voices need to be heard.

Journo: But the public opinion on this matter has been known for years. An overwhelming majority of the population support X.

Polly: Our party has a long tradition of not reacting to the whims of whatever is popular as drummed up by the spurious polls conducted by the media for mere sensationalism. We have principles, we are not a populist party.

Journo: In terms of principles, where do you stand on the matter of X?

Polly: Look, in principle we support the concept of X, but the cost of X to taxpayers is something that needs to be taken into account in any dialogue on this matter.

Journo: So principles are overridden by economics.

Polly: I didn't say that.

Journo: Didn't you? What did you say then?

Polly: Look, I have answered your questions and there are others here… Next?

Too Cool To Cancel

We come by train, bus, ferry, Uber, and on foot.

In pubs and clubs, in sandstone districts saved in the 70s by union green bans, we pre-load on beer and wine, and rum and Coke.

Illicit drugs are done in seedy bathrooms or out in the park behind the shrubbery on land stolen from native people and later cleared of 'the idle and profligate hoi polloi'.

Intoxication an absolute necessity in a world where an untainted view of reality is way too confronting for us mere mortals. We crave euphoria, a night of release from the prison of the modern anxiety state.

We funnel our way onto the finger of land transformed to the point where its namesake, a humble and smiling Gadigal man, would now be totally lost. They sailed him across the seas to the mother country and dressed him in red and white finery so as to be presentable to polished society. After he had sufficiently satisfied the curiosity of the scientific world and delighted the landed gentry, they took him back to where he belonged, the smallpox-cleansed *Terra Nullius.*

We come in droves to worship at the foot of our saviour. The irony of mass devotion to a model of unrivalled individuality is lost in the heat and thrum of a humid summer night. We line up on gaffer tape crosses stuck down on the pretty pink granite pavement. The orderly desiring disorderliness.

Positioned on the steps, with Utzon's re-engineered sails at our back, we wait. As the sun sets, the sea breeze abates and bats take to the sky.

The stage is as exactly as we imagined. The red velvet portière, through which Guy Chapman and the Holy Revelation will be born, is centre stage. The crucifix and altar are positioned stage left along with the keyboard set-up and chairs for the string section. Behind the altar, microphones for the back-up singers, the Poor Clares, who we know will be dressed, initially at least, in full habit. Stage right is the spa and cocktail bar, the domain for drums, bass and the dance troupe Legs Eleven.

Out front, centred on the apron, is a single radio-style microphone perched on its stand, Guy Chapman's pulpit.

We call him the Man. We've been following him for decades. Women, old and young, throb in his presence. Men want to be him. Guitarists ape him. In acts of permanent devotion, fans lie down for tattoos of stigmata on their hands and roses on their necks. In the 70s he was punk, the 80s a Goth, in the 90s he moved to Paris. In the 00s his wife died in a plane crash, resulting in a crisis of faith and a return to the needle. More recently, in the 10s he acted in movies and played concerts in Tel Aviv and P'yōngyang. In the pandemic, he performed online, solo, and sang dreary hymn-like ballads of matricide and piracy. Though constantly morphing to remain relevant, he has never wavered from his signature look: a body-hugging black dinner suit, crocodile leather double-strapped monk shoes, and a white silk shirt with a pearl-studded Chinese collar. His thick black hair has peppered with time, but is always long and slick and brushed back.

The Man, our preacher, flawed and dangerous.

The bright white lights bathing the congregation dim. A reverent silence falls, all attention now upon the stage. White LEDs outline the crucifix and a blue neon OPEN sign flickers into life behind the cocktail bar. Vapours of liquid nitrogen overflow from the bubbling spa. A spotlight illuminates the portière, upon which all now gaze.

The jostling crowd up front raise their arms, praying for a spraying of Guy Chapman's sweat. Holy water for us, the damned.

The Poor Clares choir and the Legs Eleven dance troupe file out through the labia of red velvet. The crowd ignites, clapping, hooting, stomping. Next, comes the Holy Revelation. Judas Bartholomew, the keyboard player, plunges into his bank of ebony and ivory releasing the opening overture of suspended chords. Billy-Boy Munroe pumps the kick drum violently, resuscitating the life-weary hearts of each and every punter. Jacques Badeaux dons his bass and bows his head. He won't play a note until it's time.

The Man, Guy Chapman, the maestro, the evergreen icon of masculinity, who miraculously remains unscathed as he sails headlong into the relentless waves of political correctness that have shipwrecked so many other beneficiaries of the Y chromosome, steps out into his cauldron of unconditional adoration.

We succumb to the collective fervour.

With his strapped-on guitar stylishly swung around and inverted on his back, the Man holds his palms together and bows to those up front, and to those up the back, and then to his left and finally right. His adoring, now sanctified, throng.

A humble man if you so choose to believe.

He wears a mask, black with a thorny red rose tracing his mouth. We all wear masks. No government has been as effective with compliance as our Guy Chapman, born in New Zealand, adopted as a son of Australia.

On with the show. We know what to expect. He delivers us our bread. Teaches us how to thrive in the chaos and uncertainty of sex and death. We are sinners, wallowing in our fallibility. Damaged and craving redemption. We are worshippers and, like him, lust for Eve, the first woman and every woman since, the incarnation of original sin. He sings of blood and retribution. Our loins rattle and hum and stir from their flaccid sleep. He kneels at the crucifix and prays to God, the vengeful and merciful Father of Christ. Us poor wretched unrequited souls, we sing and dance in hope of redemption.

We queue for the portaloos. Entombed in plastic, we imbibe the vapours of excrement infused with oestrogen, testosterone and the metabolites of intoxicants. The heady aroma of a rock concert. Inspired by the Man, as he gyrates with the choir of nuns and throws gold coins at Legs Eleven for lap dances, we pair up with strangers to indulge in acts of unspeakable immorality. For one night only, a cyclone-fenced sanctuary for sin – venal, cardinal, mortal. Years in purgatory being racked up with joy and abandon. Hell a hair's breadth away.

There is more to the story. There is always more.

Out there, published on the permanent record for all who choose to see, exists the accounts, recounts, audio files, court transcripts, opinions and confessions, of misogyny, greed, racism, ego, violence, addiction, gluttony, rape, homophobia, and mendacity. Name a sin. Name an unforgivable sin.

And yet, we forgive him. We yearn to dwell in the niche this broken man has carved out of modern society. Elsewhere, statues are torn down, dumped into boiling seas. Works of art burnt on bonfires of virtue. Music banned, lyrics rewritten. Welcome to the new millennial age of sensitivities. Yet this man, the Man, remains untouchable in his tailored cloak of uber coolness. There's not even a trigger warning.

For Guy Chapman, we invoke the rhetoric of separation of man and art.

Why for him alone? you ask.

The Man is cool. And the consumption of cool will never be denied. With consumer confidence at an all-time high, Guy Chapman, the penultimate purveyor of chic, is too cool to cancel.

Distracted? Yes, fully.

Lost? Absolutely.

Hopeful? Always. Without hope, death consumes us all.

Suffonsified? For now.

With elaborately rehearsed magnanimity, Guy Chapman and the Holy Revelation perform a three-song encore – thus sealing the deal.

The oil-slicked harbour water surrounding the concert diffracts the tungsten light of the nearby bridge into a miasma of rainbows. Five bells rang here once for a drunken man overboard.

Starting Over

On the morning of the day of settlement, she did an inspection of the property. The contract stated vacant possession.

'Don't settle unless they've done it, Emma,' her older sister said. 'They have to do it, you know. You don't want to be burdened with other people's junk. Promise me you'll say something.'

Emma knew there was lots of junk. At least, there was lots of it when she last inspected the property six weeks before, when the contracts were exchanged. She'd done a few drive-bys in the interim. But it was hard to see anything behind the overgrown front garden.

The cologne drenched agent let her into the house. All furniture, apart from a small telephone table, had been removed. And the place was clean. All good so far.

The backyard was a different story. There was broken outdoor furniture, busted garden tools, a grease-laden gas barbecue minus its gas bottle, and a forty-four-gallon drum that had been used as an incinerator or outdoor heater, or both. The clothesline was punctuated with scores of plastic and wooden pegs well past their use-by date. And in the back corner, just visible through a screen of tall weeds, sat an old rusty box trailer full of garbage.

'I thought all of this had to be taken away,' she enquired.

'Technically, yes,' said the young man. 'The problem is that the tenants claimed the trailer and other bits and pieces were here when they moved in. We checked the pre-rental inspection report and they were correct. It was a pretty cheap rental, so they never complained about it.'

'Well, shouldn't the owner deal with this?'

'The owner is in a nursing home in Mudgee. We have been dealing with his solicitor, who for some reason is in Melbourne, and that has been problematic.'

'Well, what do I do? I mean, you did tell me it would be vacant possession. All of this should be gone, that's right, isn't it?'

'You would have to advise your solicitor to postpone the settlement on the grounds of a breach of the contract.'

Emma could hear her sister inside her head, 'Don't let the agent get away with it.'

'Let's have a look inside the shed,' said Emma.

The agent eventually found the right key in the bundle he held and as he shouldered the door open, he was showered with paint flakes from the door and surrounding timber work. 'Don't think anyone's been in here for a while.'

The shed was full of stuff. Most of it stacked in cardboard boxes, from stud wall to stud wall, from concrete floor to corrugated-tin roof. Emma had no idea what to say or do. The settlement was in an office in Sydney at one twenty p.m. The solicitor employed by Emma's conveyancer would need to be informed ASAP if Emma was to postpone. And that would certainly add to the final bill. But then, allowing the settlement to go ahead and then having to pay someone to take all the junk away might actually cost more.

'Give me a moment or two to think,' said Emma to the agent.

Emma stepped out of the shed and walked around the backyard. Someone had mowed the lawn. It was an oval of acceptability carved out of the unruly garden. Large wet clumps of cut grass sat in concentric ellipses.

She would have to postpone the settlement. The hounding from her sister would not be worth it.

She took her mobile phone out of her handbag to ring the conveyancer. In a black and white flash, a bird swooped past and knocked the phone out of her hand.

'Are you OK?' asked the real estate agent, moving towards her. He picked up the phone from the grass and handed it to Emma.

The bird sang out from its perch on a timber paling fence. A pretty melody. A melody she recognised.

When she tried to ring again, the bird once again swooped. This time it clacked its beak right in her ear.

'It's a butcher-bird. They can get territorial in breeding season,' claimed the agent. 'Who are you calling?'

'I want to postpone the settlement until everything is taken away.' Well, that's what she said. She wasn't sure what she really wanted. It was more a matter of avoiding a confrontation with her sister. She couldn't bear another put-down.

Emma walked back over to the shed door to take another look inside. The butcher-bird, who she would later christen Birdie, flew over and landed on the rusted-out guttering right above Emma's head. It sang its song again. Later, Emma would recall this melody, the opening six notes of Debussy's 'The Girl with the Flaxen Hair'.

What could be in all those boxes? It could be fun opening them all up to see what I might find. Why do I worry about what my sister thinks?

While she was pondering her situation, the agent walked off towards the house and made a call back to his office. He was told by the licensed owner of the agency that under no circumstances should he allow the buyer to postpone settlement. 'It has to go through today. We need that commission. You need that commission.'

Emma didn't like the agent. He was a know-it-all. More than once he'd referred to the house as a knock-down. He wore a newsboy cap and a vest and fancied himself, she thought, as Tommy Shelby from *Peaky Blinders*. And she hated that show. Worst of all, he wore no socks. The thought of his smelly feet made her nauseous.

'I've just called the office,' he announced. 'They can't get hold of the owner on the phone. If you postpone, we can send a letter, but he never responds. You'll have to get your solicitor to contact his solicitor. This could drag on for months. I've seen it before. Don't you have a boyfriend with a ute, or somethink?'

Somethink, she thought loudly in her head. What a moron. Maybe I'm gay, and have a girlfriend with a ute. Or maybe I'm straight and single and I have my own ute, and am capable of getting rid of the junk by myself! Have you thought of that?

Emma took out her phone one more time. The bird above her dropped down off the guttering and landed on her shoulder. It sang out loudly, this time more of a shriek than a song. She brushed it away and felt it peck at the back of her hand, drawing blood.

By now, she was completely flustered. They say moving house is one of the top five stressors of modern life. Here she was with the agent and her sister having opposing viewpoints on the issue of vacant possession, and a crazy aggressive bird attacking her each time she thought she had made a decision. And now her hand was bleeding. Dripping all over the place.

The agent ushered her back inside the house and she washed her hand in the bathroom. There was some toilet paper left on the holder and she folded a pad of it to stem the bleeding. The agent announced coldly that he'd wait out the front while she made up her mind how she would proceed.

As she wandered around the rooms in the house that could be hers today, she calmed down somewhat. She visualised herself in her new abode. Happy, free, independent. Here, she could be who she wanted to be. So what did she want today? She stood at the kitchen sink, which was smeared with some last-minute cleaning product and looked out the window. It faced east and the morning sun shone on the driveway that ran down the side of the house, past the kitchen and onto to a carport out the back, where she could park after shopping and unload her groceries. In this house, she would eat whatever she wanted, and have the whole fridge to herself.

Moving in with her sister after the break-up with Peter was never a good idea. And being reminded constantly how lucky she was to have family that cared about her, and how she could stay as long as she wanted, eventually became so annoying that she did what she once said she would never do and made an appointment with the bank to get pre-approval for a ridiculously huge home loan. The price of freedom, the price of peace.

Now, what do I want? she thought. It was clear now. What she wanted was to get into this house as quickly as possible. No more living with the sister. No more having to deal with this uppity real estate agent. She would sort out the junk in the yard and all those boxes in the back shed in her own time and in her own way. There was no rush. And who knows what treasures she might find.

She rang the conveyancer. 'Have done the inspection,' she reported. 'All good to go ahead.'

The agent would be happy. Her sister would be furious, and the silent treatment would follow. Not such a bad thing actually.

The butcher-bird sang out its pretty melody. He, or she, or whatever this crazy beast was, was sitting on the side fence directly across from the kitchen window and had obviously been watching Emma as she sorted out her mind. Its head was raised to the morning sky and the fluffed-up feathers on its throat vibrated with the beautiful melody. Something has changed in its demeanour, she thought, and then laughed at herself.

'It appears you are happy too, Birdie. Is that so? Will you be my friend now?'

Big sister was furious at Emma for not insisting upon the removal of all the junk from the backyard and the shed. It didn't matter what Emma said about the situation, it never did, her sister was always right. Little sister should be thankful for someone caring about her.

'I give up, Emma,' she said before hanging up, and thus began the silent treatment. From experience, Emma knew this would last about three months. Then the sister would make contact one day as though nothing had happened and would invite herself up to see the new house.

Breathing space, thought Emma. And if she pre-prepared, she could delay the sister's visit for perhaps a month or two longer. 'Sorry, I'm going away that weekend.' Or, 'I've got the flu.'

But one day, she would come.

Next door lived Henry and Svetlana. They were a friendly couple and had moved into the area only a few months before. The area was cheap. Lots of old fibro houses, knock-downs supposedly. Henry played piano and filled the air with sweet music. Svetlana gardened and filled the air with the exotic scents of flowers and herbs. Emma chatted with them over the fence, and it was established early on that neither party would be knocking down their shacks and capitalising on the multiple occupancy zoning that allowed villas or town houses to be built.

All the while, Birdie, the butcher-bird, watched on. Thankfully, there was no more swooping or aggressive behaviour. It would mimic some of the melodies played by Henry. Svetlana swore that the nest it had made in the paperbark tree sitting on the border between their blocks was made from rosemary and other plant sprigs it had snipped off from her herb garden. There was no doubt Birdie had a certain presence.

Once she'd settled into the house, Emma decided to do something about her junked-up backyard. Henry and Svetlana helped her one weekend to fill the skip bin she'd organised. After emptying the rusty old box trailer with its perished and deflated tyres, the three of them managed, with quite considerable effort, to lift it up and get it on top of everything else they had dumped in the bin. Emma cooked her neighbours lamb shanks in red wine as a thank you for their help.

As always, Emma cooked more than was required. She had lamb shanks for lunch the next day and, with some meat still left over, she went out to see if Birdie might be interested. She sat down on the wrought-iron and timber-slatted bench seat she'd picked up from a kerbside chuck-out just up the road. She had to laugh when she dragged it down her driveway just as the skip bin turned up. Junk in, junk out. She positioned it under the paperbark tree for the filtered light and shade. It was right under Birdie's fragrant nest. As soon as she sat down with the lamb in her hand, Birdie joined her. He, or she, Emma couldn't tell, even after researching pied butcher-birds online, took the meat strand by strand straight from out of her hand. When all the meat was gone, Birdie sang 'The Girl with the Flaxen Hair'. Or, as Svetlana would refer to it, *La fille aux cheveux de lin.* However, this time, Birdie sang the whole melody and not just the opening six notes which was its usual habit. It was a truly impressive rendition that must have gone on for over two minutes.

'Svetlana, are you there? Did you hear that?' Emma called out over the fence. She wanted to know if anyone else had heard this remarkable feat. Then she remembered how Henry and Svetlana had told her the day before how they were driving up to Newcastle for a concert.

Birdie flew from the garden bench over to the shed. It perched on the rusting guttering right above the shed door and squawked at Emma. It was demanding attention. No song now, just a clear instruction to get over here and open the shed. Emma went inside to get the key. Birdie silently waited and watched. Emma was doing its bidding. She returned and unlocked the door and, as she nudged it open with her shoulder, was showered with flaking paint. She entered the stale cardboard air of the shed and Birdie followed, landing on her shoulder. Emma was used to Birdie by now. And she'd decided that it was a he. Birdie the boy butcher-bird. Sings like a bird, acts like a boy.

'Where to start, eh Birdie?' asked Emma.

Birdie answered by flying off Emma's shoulder and onto the top of a pile of four boxes in the corner of the shed. She moved over to check them out and Birdie hopped back onto her shoulder. She lifted the top box off the pile and placed it on the floor. Birdie flew back onto the pile and squawked, 'Next one.' At least that's what it sounded like.

Emma laughed. Was she going mad? Was she hearing things? Was this bird bossing her around? Was the thing actually talking?

She picked up the next box and placed it on top of the one she had put on the ground a moment before. This time,Birdie stayed on the box as she moved it. He sang his familiar refrain.

'OK, so this is the one you want me to open. I get it, Birdie, I get it.'

Birdie clacked his beaked in acknowledgement and flew back onto the original pile, which was now only two boxes high, just like the new pile he had instructed Emma to create. He watched quietly as she opened the box.

Inside, on top sat two books, hardcover blank-paged exercise books. The kind you'd use for a journal or visual diary. Flipping through, Emma noticed they were filled with handwritten lists of ingredients and numbered steps. Recipes of some sort. The writing was cursive and neat, and penned with blue ink from a fountain pen. The pages were adorned with illustrations of moons, stars, spiders, flowers and so on. Emma flicked through both books quickly, not paying too much attention to the contents. She placed them down onto the concrete floor.

'I'll have a closer look at these later, Birdie. Now, what is all this?'

The box contained an assortment of labelled apothecary jars – some made of clear glass and others amber, some full, some empty. Emma picked out a few for closer inspection. One was labelled Midnight Swamp Water, and another, Tincture of Deadly Nightshade. The third one she inspected, a clear glass jar, was simply labelled Frogs, and inside desiccated amphibians rattled around.

Birdie sang out loud. A strange song of haunting joy, a melody Emma had not yet heard from her new best friend.

Also inside the box was a dark timber tray filled with small empty amber glass vials and several pouches of soft leather tied up with tonging. There was also a collection of pipettes and droppers, a mortar and pestle wrapped in lilac velvet, tweezers, a set of brass spoons of various sizes that each contained a different-coloured gem set into the handle, and a small ornate bone-handled knife housed in a leather sheath. Emma tested the blade on her thumb. It was keen. You could easily draw blood with that, she thought.

'A witch's kit,' she announced to Birdie, who replied with a joyful chortle.

Later that night in bed, Emma had a closer inspection of the two books that came with all the witch's stuff in the box. One was titled *Love Potions,* the other *Concoctions for Everyday Problems and Problematic People*. She was automatically drawn to the second.

Three months had passed since her sister started the silent treatment, and earlier in the day Emma had received a text message. 'Hey, Sis, I'm coming up to visit this weekend.' Emma hated being called 'Sis'. And the three months of no contact had been a welcome respite. A string of text messages ensued. Emotionally triggered and therefore devoid of rational thought, Emma was caught out. All plans to delay her sister's visit flew out the window. Somehow, big sister, after inviting herself, flummoxed Emma into agreement.

Feeling stupid, feeling once again manipulated, Emma flipped through the pages, looking for a suitable concoction to solve her sister problem. She bookmarked the page titled 'Remedy for Opinionated Bedlamites'.

The next day, Birdie, who had made a habit of flying into the kitchen and perching on a breakfast stool to watch Emma cook, sang the sweetest melodies as Emma located the prescribed ingredients from the witch's box and placed them onto the bench.

She soaked some Skin of Water Skink in two drams of Tincture of Violets and grated the Bark of Olive Tree into the mix. After straining the concoction through Stocking of Harlot, she heated the filtrate in a copper beaker over the flame of a lard candle while reciting the following verse:

> Never more speak words of storm
> Be now polite, kind and warm,
> And if this irks your ugly norm
> Be silent like the winter corm.

Birdie applauded with the same haunting song of joy which Emma had only heard once before when she first found the box of tricks. 'Mission accomplished, eh Birdie?' she said out loud to her feathered friend.

As per the instructions, she stirred the mixture three times clockwise and seven times anticlockwise with the brass spoon with the deep red garnet set into its handle. After it had cooled, she decanted one dram into an amber vial and stoppered it with a cork.

All she needed to do now was to get the sister to consume three drops of the stuff. The book stated that the potion's efficacy would not be lessened if added to a cup of tea, for example.

Victoria was her name. She was tall and angular and wore a uniform that consisted of a black leather jacket over a white silk blouse, a houndstooth skirt, sheer pink stockings and black leather ankle boots. She always carried a royal red Glomesh clutch in which was carried a bottle of Penhaligon's Bluebell Eau de Parfum and a tube of Yves Saint Laurent's Rouge Pur Couture lipstick. Brands were important to Victoria. 'Yoohoo,' she would call just before the flash of black and white and red would come into view. When the wind was right, the vaporous notes of citrus and cloves would precede her arrival.

The immediate onslaught of sight, sound and smell always pressed Emma's buttons. And then there'd be the touch of Victoria's cold and hard fingers and the taste of stale flour that accompanied her over-dramatic embrace and cheek kiss. Emma's stomach would solidify while her bowels liquefied.

Victoria's visit to Emma's new house in Long Jetty started no differently. The physical assault on her senses was followed by a comprehensive lecture on what she should do, and who she should contact, and where she should shop to improve the sitting room, bedrooms, kitchen, dining room and bathroom.

On the tour outside, Victoria interrogated Emma about the junk removal. Emma answered honestly only to be told that she should have gotten Vic Lorusso to come and take it away for free.

What, in his helicopter? laughed Emma silently inside her now spinning head. She has to namedrop. She can't help herself. She drives me bonkers.

Back inside, as she put on the kettle, Emma was instructed to contact Blainey North for advice on colour, and, 'Don't forget to tell her you're my little sister.'

Emma snapped, 'How about you use the word "could" instead of "should" for a change?'

'I'm only trying to help, Emsie,' replied Victoria.

'Emsie!' she screamed. 'Have you forgotten that I specifically asked you not to call me that any more!'

'Emma, you never told me that.'

Emma extracted herself from the kitchen. She focused on the breath in the safety of her bedroom. She could hear her sister in the bathroom. The toilet flushed. The gas heater kicked in for the hot water tap over the handbasin. The vanity drawers were opened and closed. The toilet roll holder rattled. The mirrored medicine cabinet was opened and closed. Glass clinked on ceramic. Then silence. Emma sensed the reapplication of lipstick. The toilet seat was closed and the cistern flushed again.

With some regained composure, Emma returned to the kitchen. 'Would you like a cup of tea? I bought some lapsang souchong when you texted you were coming.'

'Yes, please,' replied Victoria.

A long-established pattern had just been played out. For the sake of maintaining sororal harmony, Emma's outburst would be shelved and they would sit and drink tea while Act II unfolded. Victoria would recount her latest domestic dramas and Emma would listen and, when asked, suggest solutions. Victoria would inevitably dismiss them, though later adopt them and boast about her successes and how she had conceived the very same solutions in the first place. Emma would bite her tongue and be grateful that Victoria would soon have to dash off to meet some new very special, and talented, and famous person who Emma had never heard of.

Big sister rambled on oblivious as Emma placed three drops of Remedy for Opinionated Bedlamites into Victoria's cup. She placed it down in front of her and sat down opposite with her own cup. She sipped away as she listened to Victoria go on and on about her fat and useless husband. Then she went on about men in general. Then about women in general. Then about how she would never take the vaccine and how Pete Evans had been vilified by the mainstream media which she claimed to never listened to.

'Drink your tea, Victoria, before it gets cold.'

'Actually, I'll just have a water.'

Typical, thought Emma. I should have predicted that.

Emma took Victoria's teacup away and just as she was about to tip it down the drain in the kitchen sink, she spotted Birdie out on the fence staring back at her. She tried to make sense of this moment. She was certain that the black and white bird had somehow invaded her life, entered her mind even, a kind of avian spectre. It turned up uninvited on settlement day. It harassed and pecked her. It would sing beautiful songs one moment and then in an instant, in ready judgement, squawk, or even swoop with disapproval. This bird was ruling her life. It led her to the witch's kit in the shed. And yes, that's right, that day when she cooked up the concoction for her sister, Birdie flew at her head when she mistakenly picked up the wrong spoon to stir the brew.

Staring back, right into Birdie's eyes, Emma lifted Victoria's cup of tainted lapsang souchong to her lips and drank it down in one long satisfying draught. Birdie flew straight at the kitchen window. Emma ducked instinctively. Victoria screamed out at the sound of bird skull striking the pane of glass. Birdie dropped to the ground.

By the time the sisters had calmed down after the shock and walked outside to check on the bird, ants were eating its eyes.

Some people say everything happens for a reason. Emma always struggled with this interpretation of how the world worked. She preferred the notion that things simply happened and then people made up the reasons. For example, she might reason that the recipe for Remedy for Opinionated Bedlamites was to be taken by the victim rather than the perpetrator. Alternatively, she could reason that perhaps she herself was an opinionated bedlamite, just like her sister. What do they say about birds of a feather?

Whatever happened, be it magic or coincidence, things changed that day when Birdie the pied butcher-bird smashed its skull on Emma's kitchen window. Victoria left, and has never visited again. In fact, Victoria has stopped meddling in Emma's life altogether. And, shock of all shocks, Emma spied a photo on Instagram of Victoria dressed in a sky-blue velour tracksuit.

And call it a miracle if you must, that once pesky cologne-soaked real estate agent who dressed so dandy and whatnot, called by the other day to inform Emma how real estate values had sky rocketed in recent months and that if she was interested he could list her place and guarantee a quick and profitable sale. Emma said no, she liked her home and had no intention of leaving.

'I don't blame you,' he replied. He wished her well and turned to leave without further ado. Can you believe it?

'Would you like a cup of tea?' she asked.

'Sure, why not,' he replied.

As they sat out under the paper bark tree sipping their teas while next door Henry played Bach's Air on a G String and Svetlana cut a bunch of zinnias, Emma looked at the young fellow's face and saw not an agent, but a man.

December 2020–January 2021

Tuesday, 8 December 2020

5.04 a.m.
Christmas. It's a Christian thing. Morphed and assimilated, personalised and commercialised. Seasonally appreciated, proportional to your latitude north or south. Food, a focus. Family, a necessity. Gifts, optional. Giving, the whole point.

And as we near the end of a year which has marked us all in one way and a thousand, good and bad, predictable and crazily unbelievable, we dream of what can be in 2021. Lest we forget.

Friday, 25 December 2020

5.19 a.m.
It's raining. I closed the van door and took my beach towel off the line. People, no more than ten adults, will be coming later, and if the ABC weather guy is right, all will be well.

We used to talk about the weather, now it's about climate.

We used to talk about holidays, now we talk about a virus.

We used to wonder about what we could do for the world, now we wonder what the world will do to us.

Christmas is still a time of giving, or is it?

I'll walk down to the service station later and get some ice for the esky. Remember when nothing, except hotel dining rooms for bona fide travellers, was open on Christmas Day? Remember bona fide travellers?

I have family and friends in the upper Northern Beaches lockdown zone. They won't be coming to my place as planned. We are planning now for a January Christmas, that is if Linda can get back from Queensland after Jetstar cancelled all flights from 26 December to 8 January. The Avalon cluster has crossed the border from New South Wales into Queensland, so who knows what might happen?

We used to plan for the future. Now we take it as it comes. We never stop learning, hopefully.

Some of us have had an absolutely terrible 2020. Some of us have barely noticed a difference. The notion that we are all in this together has been proven to be a bona fide lie.

The spirit of Christmas, the spirit of giving, is the spirit of humanity. It doesn't matter what day of the year, it matters every day.

Saturday, 2 January 2021

7.14 a.m.
Everyone's wanting, hoping, praying that 2021 will be better than 2020. Hope. The futility of hope. Hope means wishing that the external world will behave more kindly. Wishful thinking. Is hope is just another form of desire?

Wednesday, 13 January 2021

7.16 a.m.
The US of A is on tenterhooks in the lead-up to the inauguration of Joe Biden next week. It's fascinating stuff. The world's number one economy on the brink of chaos.

It's hard to know what should be done when people don't accept the outcome of an election, especially when they have no qualms about storming the halls of government and are prone to take up arms.

A basic tenet of democracy is that the outcome of the vote has to be accepted by those who didn't vote for that outcome. It's a rule of the game. We educate our children about it from an early age. I can't help but seeing Trump and his followers as children who haven't learnt a basic lesson of life.

The blocking of Trump and others from certain social media sites has been decried as censorship, an assault on free speech. It is no such thing. Social media sites are publishing platforms and therefore free to decide what and who they publish.

Sunday, 17 January 2021

4.19 a.m.

The other day, a politician told a lie, a big porky pie. It wasn't the first time, and it won't be the last. But for some deluded fools, this was absolute and irrefutable evidence confirming that alien reptile-like creatures have installed themselves on Earth and teamed up with Bill Gates and a paedophile ring to control the world through the creation of a fake virus.

Thursday, 21 January 2021

6.00 a.m.

I got up at three this morning. I watched the inauguration on television and now am in my office to drinking coffee and reading news. Like Michael Moore, I want Trump in jail.

Sanctum Sanctorum

The newly inaugurated president of the United States, Joseph Robinette Biden Junior, stands alone in the empty Oval Office. The furniture, the paintings, the drapery and the oval rug have been removed. Joe is not a superstitious man, but he means to get a fresh start, in every way.

The polished oak and walnut parquetry floor reflects the three tall windows in front of which will sit the desk from where the president will lead the nation. After an arduous and frightening lead-up to this day, Joe relishes a rare moment of peace.

There is a knock at the door. It's Kamala and Cedric. Joe is expecting them. Not for decorating tips – Joe has left that to Jill, his second wife, now the first lady. Jill has employed her daughter Ashley to assist. No money is changing hands in this arrangement. The Bidens are all too well aware of the absolute propriety required by this office.

Joe briefly thinks about his first wife, Neilia, and daughter, Naomi, who were killed in an automobile accident, so long ago now. He wishes they could be here, but he's not superstitious, they are just memories. Nice memories, sad memories.

Though a Catholic, a practising one at that, Joe doesn't really believe in God, or saints, or the virgin birth, heaven, nor hell. Like many Catholics, and presidents, he goes through the motions. God bless America! He can justify to himself that Christianity is as good a moral philosophy as any other. Asking himself what Jesus would do has been handy in sticky situations. And there have been plenty of those in Joe's half century of public life.

Joe snaps back to the moment and gently jogs over to the bespoke curved door to receive his vice president and senior advisor. 'It would be nice to have a group hug,' says Joe as he points out an elbow.

Not only because of the fiasco of the Rose Garden super-spreader event, and the consideration of his age, but because Covid-19 has devastated so many families in the USA, Joe is determined to beat the pandemic and to lead by example.

But the pandemic is not on the agenda today. Joe simply wants to spend some personal time with his two closest colleagues who he hopes will be his most loyal allies.

'You both know I've had Johannes schedule morning sessions, Monday, Wednesday and Fridays, just for the three of us. At these times, in this room, I want you always to be totally honest with me. I want you to know that these sessions are open to whatever needs to be discussed. They are essentially to deal with the most pressing issues. Even if the issue is a personal one. We are mere humans, and if a family member is sick, or you yourself are not feeling fit, let's share it. Let's make this place, at those times, a safe place, a place where we can confidently and implicitly trust and support each other.'

Kamala and Cedric look at each other and smile. They know Joe, they know he means it.

There is another knock at the door.

'Yes, come in,' calls Joe.

It is Johannes, the chief of staff. He leads in a small team of workers who set up trestle tables and chairs. The tables are quickly covered with starched white tablecloths, and morning tea is laid out. The main feature being a large oval fruit platter.

Johannes explains how the fruit platter has been gifted to the president by the Young Democrats of America. Red, white and blue concentric rings of fruit – raspberries, star-shaped slices of apple, and blueberries – surround a single whole uncut orange which sits on a pedestal in the centre. A small blue flag, inscribed with some handwriting in gold ink, is planted in the top of the orange.

Kamala pulls out the flag and reads to herself, 'For Biden, Fruit!' She can't help but let out a small chuckle.

'What does it say?' asks the president.

She shares the message and hands the flag to Cedric. They both look at Joe to see his reaction.

'For Biden, Fruit,' he repeats. 'Mmm…'

Johannes ushers the hospitality staff out of the office, and exits himself.

'Let's sit,' says Joe.

They take their seats and Joe picks up a knife and a large plate, which he sets down in front of himself. 'OK, one more point. Whatever happens in this office with the three of us, stays in this office, agreed?'

'Agreed,' is the response in unison.

Joe leans over, takes the orange from the centre of the platter, positions it on the plate, and slices it in half. The centre of the orange is blood red and juice spills out onto the white plate.

'Mmm,' says Joe again.

Kamal and Cedric wait.

Like a priest at mass preparing the Eucharist, Joe cuts each half into half again and places a quarter orange on each of three smaller plates. He carefully positions a neatly folded white linen napkin on each plate and passes them to his guests.

In reverential silence, Kamala and Cedric sit with arms resting in their laps. They wait.

Joe takes the leftover quarter of the blood orange with two hands, and without taking his eyes off it, raises it above his head. 'The body and blood of Trump.'

Now the president waits. Still there is silence. No response from his compatriots.

'This is when you say, amen.'

The vice president and the senior advisor utter an unsure 'Amen'.

Joe breaks out in laughter. He recovers from the mirth. 'Relax, it's OK. I'm joking. Let's eat this fruit, and Cedric, can you please pass my regards onto the Young Democrats. With folk like them, I'm feeling evermore positive about the future.'

Circa 2041

It has been months since the last transmission from Earth. The general consensus is that modern civilisation has been completely destroyed by the world war which we observed from our base on the Moon. Now we must become totally self-sufficient. There is no chance of any supplies coming from Earth in the foreseeable future, if ever.

Before the storm of nuclear flashes, it was clear something was wrong. Ground control tried to shield us from the increasing international tensions that were building at the time. And I am certain they had told our partners and family members not to mention anything about domestic affairs. But I knew something was awry. I could see it my husband's face. I could hear the fear in his voice. And where on Earth did he get that twitch from? Earth is where he got it. Anytime I asked about what was going on back on terra firma, his left eye would blink uncontrollably. Or was it intentional, a signal to alert me?

Whether or not anyone is still alive on Earth is a topic of discussion strongly discouraged by our commander. Thankfully, I don't have children. My post-war nightmares are bad enough. Disturbing images of burning flesh and the sounds of screaming wake me more nights than not. The commander is right, we need to focus on our own survival. The members of the mission with children back on Earth are the ones struggling the most. We are not returning to Earth as planned. Our shift has changed from a twelve-month contract to permanent. The medical team are rationing the Xanax.

I work in communications. Oddly, the head of my team died an hour before the world ended. He was found in his room, wrists slit. It looked like suicide but, as per protocol, an autopsy was immediately triggered. But then, the atmosphere on Earth caught fire. At least that is what it looked like from here. In the large common area, a clear geodesic dome where we eat and relax, we stood in disbelief and watched. There were screams and crying, and weirdly, a lot of us started moving around in circles not knowing what to do even though knowing all too well there was absolutely nothing that could be done. It was the middle of our long lunar night, it was a waning gibbous Earth and the fireworks lasted less than four hours.

Now, I woman the radio receiving room. Listening to a silent Earth. I look through the telescope that is pointed permanently at Earth. A small motor imperceptibly moves the equatorial mount. Strangely, Earth looks exactly the same. Humankind wipes itself out and the planet gets on with what it gets on with. I imagine it gets on with the breaking down of toxic nuclear waste. I wonder about the plants and animals, and what would be going on in the oceans.

I feel useless. Others are working full tilt at designing and setting up oxygen, water and food systems, and I sit in the coms room. Once an hour, I transmit a recorded message made by our commander in the hours after the war. Even though it is sent at scores of frequencies within the S, X, and Ka bands, the whole process involves exactly eleven point and clicks of my mouse. Then I don the headphones and listen to the static at 145.80 MHz. The computer listens to all other frequencies.

Last night, an artificial night that is – set in sync with Washington DC – I had a dream that I heard, in amongst the static, Elvis Presley singing 'Suspicious Minds'. I woke up in a sweat and was panting. I thought about my husband. Was there any chance he was alive? Any chance that anyone was alive? I forced myself to do the breathing exercises that had become a mandatory part of our daily prescribed well-being program. I did manage to fall back asleep, only to toss and turn to a backdrop of unsettling dreams I can't even begin to describe.

Dr Basim Haniff asks to sit with me as I quaff coffee in the common room. I point at a chair to accept. I glance up at Earth – currently a waxing crescent, hard to ignore such beauty. Basim is a good guy. I remember in the training camp for this mission how he handled the racists. He copped it from men and women, from engineers and other medicos, from the lowest ranks and even from the commander on one occasion. He would smile and then respond in a way that would make the subtle racism obvious. The offender would then have to back-pedal in some clumsy attempt to prove that they weren't really racist after all. It was fun to watch. Unfortunately, though, Basim made some enemies for simply, and rightly, refusing to cop it sweet.

One day in a team-building exercise, this haughty female lieutenant, when introduced to Basim, announced for all to hear, 'My cousin married a Basim. He makes the best kebabs.'

Basim smiled. 'Is that so, Debbie. Whenever I hear your name, I always think of that chimpanzee on *Lost in Space*. Remember that show?'

I couldn't help but say out aloud, 'Touché!' Basim has been my confidant ever since.

'How are you going?' I ask.

'Yeah, well...still can't get my head around all this. My dreams are crazy. How are you?'

We talk for a while, nothing serious, though everything is serious. Then he smiles, and I reciprocate. It's good to have a friend up here.

'The autopsy has been done, finally.'

'Really? What's the verdict?'

'Officially...' Basim looks around and determines it is safe, 'suicide.' And he gives me this look saying it wasn't suicide at all.

'You're kidding,' I say while looking around.

'I wish I was.'

Imagine the planning needed to put twelve hundred people onto the Moon for a year. Then imagine the political stability needed for a project that would end up spanning five presidential terms. Biden '21 to '25, Harris '25 to '33, and then Ocasio-Cortez, '33 to '41. An unprecedented Democratic era. Then in 2041, the return of Trump, Ivanka this time, and the return of the all new gung-ho GOP. How she won had many of us scratching our heads. My grandmother said it was the same when her father, Donald, won in 2016. Unbelievable. Fortunately, our mission was too big to fail, like the banks back in 2008. Like democracy in 2020. Well, so I've read.

But all of this is history, and for all intents and purposes it appears that history has ended. There has not been a peep from Earth. I imagine soon I will be relieved of listening out for any signs of life. I've been given training modules in advanced lunar horticulture to complete. I heard rumours that someone smuggled coffee plant seeds in their personal kit. It was against all regulations and the culprit was punished. But since the end of the world, the smuggler's contraband has been hailed as a godsend. Only twelve months supply of coffee was shipped up before we arrived. It was never planned to grow coffee here. We do grow fresh herbs and fruits and vegetables, and we have chickens and pigs and fish for meat. Tea, coffee, milk powder, candy, nicotine, antibiotics and many other needs are stored in bulk, to be replenished by supply modules launched from Earth. We do make ethanol, and its consumption was, until now, strictly regulated. Though people did work out ways around that. But I digress. I'm bored and ready to grow coffee plants. The emergency geodesic greenhouses have been constructed and our used coffee grounds mixed into moon dirt is proving to be a suitable medium for germination. I suspect I'll be reassigned soon. I don't know how much more static I can listen to.

Someone taps me on the shoulder. I jump in my seat and rip off my headphones. It's Basim.

'I wish you wouldn't do that,' I say as I catch my breath.

'I did call out,' Basim explains. 'Have you looked at the captain's log?'

Basim is on my case. He is certain that, somewhere, evidence exists that will lead us to uncovering the identity of the murderer. Yes, we have a murderer. We had a smuggler and now we have a murderer. It appears that no amount of psych testing done in the selection process stopped criminals getting up here onto the Moon. Who knows what other types of undesirables we are living with. Thieves? Rapists?

'The only unusual thing I've found is that Captain Wilson left his post at 12.14. One hour before the war began. Three hours before his rostered finish time. I can't imagine why he would do that.'

'Helen, he must have been drugged here and led back to his room and killed.'

'Basim, I don't want to think about it. Flunitrazepam? You said that what was what in his blood? Rohypnol? The date rape drug?'

'Yes, Helen, yes!' Basim is frustrated with me.

I can't blame him. I have been in a state. Frozen in denial. I don't want to believe everyone on Earth is dead. I don't want to believe we have a murderer in our midst. And I don't want to believe Basim's theory that the murder of Captain Wilson was somehow connected to the starting of the thermonuclear war we witnessed from our bubble on the moon.

Basim leaves after I reassure him that I will do some further searching for evidence. I'm sick of listening to 145.8, so I turn on the scanner. At least different frequencies have different statics. Ground control would have been a target. The radio silence from there will surely be permanent. Perhaps a survivor somewhere is broadcasting something on a longer wavelength. The algorithm in our supercomputer wouldn't have the same auditory discrimination as a human ear. Maybe I will hear something. Some small sign that human life persists on Earth. Imagine hearing REM's 'It's the End of the World as We Know It (And I Feel Fine)' being broadcast from some bunker down under in Australia or New Zealand.

I pull up Wilson's log again. His last entry, 11.57 a.m.:

> Ground control advise of impending outage due to maintenance. Have relayed information through to relevant channels here on base. Anticipate frustration for folks with telecons booked with family and loved ones. It's clear things aren't great back home. China and US at loggerheads again. New POTUS certainly talking tough.

Then nothing. Just the metadata indicating that Wilson logs off at 12.14:47 [GMT-5] 6/22/41. The official story states he then retires to his cabin to slit his wrists. Of course that is false. I knew Wilson well. He talked often about his family and how this would be his final mission. 'I'm going to teach my grandson how to fly-fish for trout in the Frying Pan River.'

Basim is right. Wilson was murdered. Why? And who? And what could this have to do with the end of the world as we know it?

After work and study, I swim laps. It helps my sanity. The physical exercise a bonus. The warm water flowing over my skin soothes my existential misery. Though we have been instructed, encouraged, distracted and even rewarded to not think or talk about life on Earth, it happens.

And talk flows at the pool. Basim swims as well, and yesterday he apologised for pressuring me. We were up the deep end in the medium pace lane. As we were talking, a swimmer in the fast lane next to us pulled up and swiped off her goggles. She was breathing heavily and looked up through the clear roof to Earth, which was shining in last quarter. We ignored her and kept chatting.

'Have you heard about the coffee seedlings?' Basim asked.

'Well, I've heard there have been issues with some sort of fungal infection.'

'Looks like when the stockpile runs out, that'll be the end of one more drug. You know there's only a month's supply left of Xanax.'

'Well, looks like alcohol will be our only sustainable vice.'

'Long live our livers!' Basim chuckles.

'I don't now how you can laugh, Basim.'

I dunked under the water and resurfaced. The girl in the fast lane was looking at us. I had seen her before. And so had Basim. In the cafeteria, soon to be coffeeless, we had commented on the way she walked and held herself.

'Full of herself. A Trumpist for sure,' said Basim.

'I thought they got weeded out in the selection process.'

'Unfortunately no. A last-minute executive order placed a smattering of loyal Trumpists into our ranks.'

I was embarrassed to be so naive about politics. I was, at the time of the change of presidency, so focused on the mission ahead that I tuned out of current affairs. Steven, my husband, was expressing concern and occasionally screaming at the television, but I chose to ignore all the noise. I needed to get my head around a year away from everything Earth.

'Are you going to the dance party?' asked the girl in the lane next to us.

I suggested maybe. Basim answered no. He was cynical about the efforts of the upper echelons to reward us for forgetting the nuclear annihilation of civilisation and getting on with the survival of the species.

'If you come, I have some eccys. It's not what you know but who you know, if you know what I mean.'

With that, she turned and pulled herself up and out of the pool. We both noticed the red Q tattooed on her right hip. Basim looked at me and opened his eyes wide.

I said, 'I know what that tattoo stands for. You don't have to explain that. I'm not that naive.'

The girl was a Trumpist. And she had access to MDM. I don't know why, but I felt certain she was somehow linked to Wilson's murder.

'I'm going,' I said to Basim. 'I could use some hypnotic beats and drug enhancement to ease my mind.'

'Have fun. I couldn't stand all the posturing.' Basim left the pool.

I ducked under the lane rope into the fast lane and swam six laps at full pelt.

It's open bar tonight. Ethanol production has been ramped up. It does have many uses. Tonight it's a solvent. Dissolving our sadness and survivor guilt. Helping us to overcome the feeling we have no right to party.

The beats are loud, pulsing through our chests. There must be close to a thousand of us here. A throbbing mass with its arms up in the air.

The girl from the pool spots me. She dances her way over and embraces me. I knew she was gay. I didn't say anything to Basim at the pool, but her tone and the way she directed the invitation at me was telling.

I also didn't say anything to Basim about my sense that this girl was connected to Wilson's murder. I'm not here to get pissed and off my head on ecstasy. I'm here to find out what this girl knows. Tonight, I will play the heteroflexual older woman.

'I don't know your name,' I yell into her ear as we dance.

'Penny,' she replies. Her hot breath in my ear. 'And you are Helen. I've done my research.'

We dance. Some others join in. A circle forms, Penny next to me. She grabs my hand and manoeuvres a capsule into my palm. I feign gratitude with a smile.

The song ends and people move off.

I whisper in Penny's ear, 'Thanks, I'm going to go get a water.'

At the bar, I look back to see if Penny is watching. She is. I pop the capsule into my mouth for her benefit. For my benefit, I place it under my tongue and take a swig of water and wash nothing down my throat. I turn back to the bar, order two Hirohitos, and secretly spit the capsule back into my hand then slip it into my mini Glomesh handbag. I pull out my e-cig and take a large apple-flavoured nicotine hit. The drinks are ready and I dance my way back to Penny, holding the cocktails aloft.

'I didn't at first take you for a party animal.' Penny sips her cocktail.

'Grrr,' I purr.

I finish the rum and sake cocktail in one draught. I know I can handle my alcohol. Though saying that, my year on the moon was in part meant to be a kind of self-enforced break from an escalating drinking habit that my husband had noticed and occasionally commented upon. Little did I know that World War III would erupt and that alcohol would be officially sanctioned by management to help ease the troubled souls of us so-called New Frontier Pioneers. Basim and I would secretly joke about how patronising and shallow the mission propaganda was. We knew, as did many others, that most of us joined the mission purely for financial reasons. Who wouldn't pretend to be patriotic and philosophical about humanity's destiny to colonise space when the promise of an end to crippling personal debt was on offer? And everyone had debt. The fiat currency Ponzi scheme started in the 1970s was still running hot even after twenty years of Democratic reform. Children born after 2030 were born in debt. Crazy.

Penny follows my lead and skulls her Hirohito. She grabs my hand and we are back out on the dance floor. I close my eyes and let the heavy beats pulse through me. I offer no resistance to Penny's touching, though in my head I wonder what the hell I am getting myself into.

After one ten-minute techno song, though how it could be called a song I have no idea, Penny whispers loudly in my ear and invites me back to her pod.

I nod and submit. She leads me towards the main exit. I act drug-affected, but gaze around to see who might be watching me being led away by this Trumpist who has researched my name.

I recount the events to Basim. 'We were on her bed. We'd done a few things and then she wanted me to take my dress off. I sat up and said, "I'm sick of being up here, wondering who is still alive on Earth and what is going on down there. This base is doomed, surely. What happens when we run out of supplies that we can't produce up here? I'd do whatever it takes to get back to Earth. Surely there's other people alive. Surely there's safe places to live."'

Basim looks into my eyes. I look down, embarrassed.

'So you didn't just go to let off some steam? You were probing, investigating. Proud of you, Hels.'

'Well, I'm not proud of me. Especially as I fucked up. I was too upbeat, too concerned about stuff, obviously not on MDM.'

'So what happened?'

'I noticed Penny starting to get suspicious. I panicked a bit and thought I'd better try to get some info, anything before she'd cotton on that I was a fake lesbian, or worse. I asked her, "Do you think the president and her family are alive?" Then she sat up and said, "We know they are. And we will join them soon. But you won't need to worry about any of that." "What do you mean?" I asked. Now I was really getting worried.

'Then she said, "You didn't swallow the capsule, did you?" Her face said it all. I jumped up off the bed and headed for the door. She lunged at me and grabbed me from behind in a bear hug. I elbowed her in the ribs and as she gasped for air I was able to squirm free. Then I remembered my handbag. I moved to get it from off her sideboard and she lunged at me again. This time, I managed to get my elbow into her face. Her teeth stabbed into my arm. See?' I show Basim my wound.

'Anyway, I got the bag and stormed out of the door into the hallway. But two men were there, waiting. One to my left, one to my right. I was blocked. Penny called out from inside her pod, "Get her!" Fortunately, just as they moved in to grab me, a party of four came into the hallway. They were drunk and loud. The two men stopped and tried to pretend nothing was going on. One of them tried to engaged in light conversation. I noticed one of the group was Bridget, you know her.'

'Yes, Bridget,' says Basim.

'I said hello to her and she says, "Hey, Helen, what's going on?" "I'm heading home," I said. "I've had too many Hirohitos. Hey, could you do me a favour and come with me to my pod?" Then one of the he-men interjects and says that Bridget needn't worry, that she could go on with her party mates and that he would kindly escort me home. I pushed him in the chest and mockingly said, "No, I don't need some boofhead shining white knight! Bridget can take me home." I quickly moved over to Bridget and grabbed her hand and began to walk away. Bridget got the picture, and excused herself from her friends. I don't know what would have happened if Bridget and her friends hadn't come along.'

'Well,' says Basim, 'you're here now, and safe.'

'There was no way I was going to go back to my pod. Those two goons would have gone there for sure. The Trumpists had not finished with me, especially now that I had found out from Penny how a mission back to Earth is planned. I guess when you lick a red Q tattoo on a drunken girl's hip and lie to her how you admire Ivankya Trump, you get what you ask for.'

Basim's laptop signals an email. It's the results from the tox-screen of the capsule Penny gave me.

'Well, it's not MDM,' says Basim. 'It's Rohypnol, same isomer that was found in Captain Wilson.'

I feel a panic attack coming on. Basim sits down in front of me, holds my hands, and guides my breathing.

Basim calls a friend in security. 'Ari, it's Basim. I need a favour. My friend and I need to get safely out of my pod.'

The conversation continues, arrangements are made.

I wonder what they want from me. Do they think I have found out what Captain Wilson had found out? Found out whatever it was that led to him having to be eliminated. Was I to be eliminated? And what could that knowledge be?

If the Trump administration were alive and well, had they initiated World War III? And what is their plan and how are the Trumpists on the moon base involved? What did Wilson find out? And why have people in the upper ranks created an official story that Wilson killed himself? Is there a Trumpist or two in the inner circle? Are they orchestrating this mission back to our war-ravaged planet to rejoin the president and her allies in some engineered post-apocalyptic future world? It does seem as though they are prepared to eliminate anyone in their way.

Basim hangs up the intercom handset. 'It's all sorted.'

I feel a wave of relief wash over me. Then I realise I am in a party dress and bare-footed. I grasp my Glomesh mini handbag to my chest. Basim laughs and pulls a coverall out from his wardrobe.

Earth is waxing last quarter and it is a lunar night. Basim and I are in the tranquillity lounge watching our beautiful blue planet. Our home. After we got into the safety of the security wing and I told my story, and Basim handed over the real autopsy results for Wilson, events unfolded quickly. Penny was arrested, and interrogated after being given a dose of LSD. She spilled the whole story. The Trumpists were rounded up and detained in a large detached geodome that was, thanks to the absence of a lunar atmosphere, completely isolated and thus totally secure. They were put to work growing and harvesting coffee beans.

The best news of all is that radio transmissions from Earth have started up. There are survivors. I was right, they are in Australia and New Zealand, but also in Chile and Argentina, and parts of Africa. There have also been transmissions from Scandinavia and the very northern parts of Canada. The US and Europe including the UK are still silent. We will be going home. Not straight away. The date and the landing location are yet to be determined. There are many factors, radiation levels being just one.

The Trumps on Earth are housed in a massive underground complex. It is locked and secured by a labyrinth of fail-safe mechanisms. The Trumpists on the Moon possess the encrypted digital holographic keys to release the occupants who mistakenly believe they are the only people on Earth who would have survived the holocaust of World War III which they started. The commander has assured us the imprisoned Trumpists will be the only New Frontier Pioneers to become permanent residents of the Moon.

I have resigned myself to the overwhelming likelihood that my husband, Steven, perished in the nuclear inferno. Basim, and everyone else here, is dealing with the same. We are a community bound by grief. But also we share an emerging hope and promise for our future.

Basim raises his cocktail glass to toast our planet. Tonight we are having Blue Lagoons. I have given up Hirohitos, they leave a bad taste of Penny in my mouth.

February 2021

Tuesday, 23 February 2021

5.55 a.m.

All The Pretty Places

The ones you see on apps on your phones

The blue skies, the beaches, the mountains, the old buildings, the weather-beaten locals, the cuisine

The places now spoiled by influencers

The influencers, the distractors, the dream makers, the gurus of anything is possible

The influencers, the latest iteration of snake oil salespeople

Wednesday, 24 February 2021

6.54 a.m.

It's Not Rocket Science, or Is It?

I'm in the middle of a bureaucratic goose chase with a government department. It's hair-pulling-out stuff. I have supplied said department with the exact same information through five different channels and still, somehow, the situation has not been resolved to the bureaucracy's satisfaction. It's a hungry machine, devoid of empathy. It's a Tower of Babel!

I'm not surprised that people vote for politicians who tout less regulation and smaller governments – private enterprise and the free market are the solution for a smoother ride – NOT!

I say this because I also find myself on an insane merry-go-round ride with my telecommunications/energy provider. Ironically, a government website helped me to find this particular provider! We've all heard how you have to shop around to get the best deal.

Saying that, have you shopped around to find a better bank deal? I mean, you'd have to be a fool to be paying the fees you are currently paying. Get on the phone and barter with your bank. And if they don't come to the party, just change your bank. Easy peasy, get online, get on the phone and change everything.

Currently, I'm trying to get out of my community bank – yes, one that's not even for profit. I have one share and two accounts with this credit union. Their online banking service often goes down. Once, I had to download a whole new web browser to access my accounts. My regular browser was no longer compatible! And now, as I try to escape, I have to contact all these government departments and private enterprises, including my telecommunications/energy provider, who has a 'bundle' of my services, and also my numerous employers (if you can call the businesses who hand out gigs through apps on mobiles, employers), including one which doesn't respond to emails and doesn't even have a phone number. Yeah, change your bank, it's easy – NOT!

The other day on the phone after listening to menu after menu of options that didn't fit my situation, I finally pressed # and spoke to an operator. Feeling like I had made some serious progress, I felt I had no choice but to accept their request, 'Can you please hold?' Then, while listening to an endless thirty-second loop of infuriating muzak, I realised that the navigation of hostile worlds requires a team of experts. I emailed NASA and asked, 'Now that you have successfully landed Perseverance on Mars, do you have some spare time to assist me with some wicked problems I have encountered here on Earth?'

The Big House

It's not illegal. He'd heard that once or twice as an excuse for bad behaviour. His father once declared, after being caught in flagrante delicto with the woman next door, 'Adultery is not a crime, son.' He'd even heard the prime minister quote the rule of law to excuse what many of us would regard as criminal.

But growing marijuana is illegal. And for that he was caught. A commercial quantity, though he never intended to sell it. It was for him and his mates, with enough left over to make some cannabis oil to give to his mother and any other terminal cancer patient who needed it.

But the law is the law, and for this offence, jail time was mandatory.

Day one, he met Mad Dog.

'Welcome to the Big House. What you in for?'

'Growing dope.'

'Musta been a shitload.'

'Yeah.'

Mad Dog was in for a long stint. Vehicular manslaughter. 'Hold your head up, boy. Never look down. Look down and before you know it, you'll be some areshole's arsehole.'

Mad Dog was big and illustrated. He was left alone. A privilege he gained by knocking out the teeth of a mouthy lieutenant who belonged to one of the top dogs. Young Grant had Buckley's chance of staying safe by similar methods.

In the privacy of their cell after the bell, Mad Dog confessed, 'The mad bastard tough guy bullshit, it's all an act. Pure survival. I've become a Christian. I'm going to become a preacher when I get out. Do you believe in God, son?

Grant wasn't sure what to say. He certainly didn't want to disappoint his massive cell mate. Then he recalled the advice of Susan, his lawyer. Be one hundred per cent honest. It won't get you out of a custodial sentence, but it might reduce its length.

'No.'

'Good on you, son. An honest answer. It says a lot about a man.'

They shook hands. Grant relaxed for the first time that crazy day.

'By the way, my name's Colin. But outside of here you call me Mad Dog. OK?'

'OK.'

Grant climbed up onto the top bunk. It was agreed, due to his bulk, best that Colin stayed on the bottom.

'When you meet the chaplain, you might be persuaded to change your mind about God. But then again you might not. I believe in Jesus as the son of God. But there's more than one way to salvation. Not that the hardcore fundamentalist Christians accept that. They love to quote John 14:6. You know, the I am the way and the truth and the life. No one comes to the Father except through me rubbish. I reckon Jesus didn't actually say that. It wasn't his style. Jesus was humble. John wrote it, and apparently he was bit of a dickhead. I prefer a more practical approach. A life of service to others. And I'll tell you something else, some of the best men here in the Big House are Muslims. You'll find out. Meanwhile, keep your head up.'

'Thanks, Colin.'

'Here, take these, my spare pair.' Mad Dog passed some earplugs up to Grant. 'You'll need 'em. Some poor fuckers in here scream bloody murder all night long.'

Two years, eighteen months with good behaviour. The days went slow. Not a lot to do, a lot of waiting. Stand there. Line up here. Move along. Back to cells.

'Think about it, son. What is waiting? It's standing or sitting and doing nothing. If a person can't wait, how can they hope to do anything at all. Think about it.' Mad Dog made a lot of sense, a lot of the time. And time was aplenty.

Drugs were also aplenty. They came in via all sorts of ingenious ways. But under the wing of Mad Dog, Grant stayed clean. The first three weeks were hard. Grant had been a pothead and a pisspot as well. He never thought of himself as an addict, but then he never really did much thinking. His sole focus was numbing a deep and malignant edginess that smouldered inside of him. He thought of himself as a freak, the only person in the world who suffered as he did. Listening to Mad Dog each night as they retired after the bell, he discovered that he was not alone at all. Mad Dog once had a raging drug and alcohol habit, and he had a violent father. Self-destructive, reckless, and off his head, one night Mad Dog wiped out a family of four on the M1.

'Some people say I turned to God only to get out of going to hell. But that ain't true, Grant. If the big fella upstairs in the real Big House, and let me tell you this here ain't no Big House no matter what any wannabe tough guy here claims, if anything it's a sad and sorry house of lost souls, but on the bright side its the perfect opportunity to find yourself, and I hope you do that, son, that is find yourself, because when you get out, mate, it's going to be go go go again, you know what it's like out there, not a moment to think properly about things, that's why we end up in here, well, one reason why we do. Anyway, where was I, oh yeah, if God judges my sins as mortal and I am condemned to an eternity in hell, I'll accept it and go there at least with a certain amount of peace and love inside meself. Because that's the real hell, Grant, whether you're dead or alive, hell is really what burns inside of ya. The self-loathing and the hatred. I reckon Jesus really meant that the only way to heaven was along the pathway of love. Fuck knows it's taken me a few years to find some love for myself, young fella. And I still struggle. Pretty sure some nights I scream out in pain and guilt for what I did. Do I scream out, Grant? Have you heard me in the night? Be honest, mate, let me know. Have you heard me scream at all?'

'I've never heard you scream, Colin.'

'Honest?'

'Honest.'

'Apparently, I use to howl. Like a dingo, the Aboriginal fellas reckoned. That's how I got Mad Dog. You didn't hear any howling, did ya?'

'Well, now that you mention it,' said Grant, looking to see how his cell mate reacted.

Colin Mad Dog Wilson, ten years with a non-parole period of eight, looked at Grant with big circle eyes. A giant hulk of a man looking like a frightened child. 'Really?'

'No, just kidding. Sorry, Colin, didn't mean to upset you.'

Colin laughed. 'You had me going there for a moment, young fella. Good on ya. Don't worry yourself about upsetting me. I can handle it, or at least should be able to handle it. And even if I do still occasionally howl in the night, or inside my head when I think about the family I killed, especially when I picture the two young daughters, I have to accept that suffering. Have to let it be, let it wash through me and never bury it, or hide it.'

Grant had never met a man like Colin. In fact, he had never even thought for a moment that men, real men, could have a soft side, or a philosophical side. Sure, there were some male teachers at high school who weren't that macho. But they were teachers, not real men out in the real world. And then there was Mr Simpson, the school counsellor, who tried to help when the school found out that Grant's mother was being battered and bruised by an alcoholic father. Grant liked Mr Simpson, but the other boys called him a pedo. And there was Grant, all of fifteen years, stunted by a world where men were expected to be tough and deal with shit. Not talk about it, especially talk about feelings. Just fucking get on with it and do something. Fight back, get wasted, piss off, start again.

Three months into his sentence, Grant was offered a place in the Wednesday music class. The teacher was Muz, a perpetually smiling surfy dude from Maroubra who had this crazy spring in his step. First lesson, he handed Grant a guitar and helped position his stiff fingers into an E major chord. Everytime Muz winked his way, Grant was to strum.

After the blues in E warm up, Muz informed the class that the newbie's name was Grant.

The drummer, a tall skinny Aboriginal man, stood up. 'Is dat your first name, bra, or last name? Like our Unc? Uncle Stan Grant?'

The class burst out in laughter, which Grant soon found out was a major feature of Wednesday music class. From that moment, his jail nickname became Stan. The class was mainly full of Aboriginal men who were quick to laugh, and surprising to Grant, warm and humble and totally accepting of the new boy, Mad Dog's cell mate, the skinny white pothead.

'How was your first class?' asked Muz.

'Great.' Grant could not get the smile off his face. Which was of some concern since Mad Dog had told him, early on in the game, not to smile when out in the mess, or in the yard, or wash house.

'Some upstart will try to prove himself by permanently wiping the smile off your face. Poker face is best. At least until you find your feet.'

Though always graded in the bottom classes at school, Grant was a quick learner in the Big House, or the House of Lost Souls as Mad Dog had christened it. He slotted into the routines and behaved appropriately in each setting. Though always on guard in the general areas, he could relax in his cell with Colin, and in Muz's music class. Out in the main yard, 'Stan' was taught by Henry 'Tropico' Miller, a Gomeroi man, how to kick an AFL football properly. Grant wondered what his mates would think: learning music and hanging out with black fellas. But really, Grant couldn't care less. Mad Dog was right, this was a house of lost souls, and it was an opportunity, a chance to find oneself.

Day two hundred and seventeen. Heading back to their block after music class, Grant and the others were stopped by two screws blocking the walkway. They could see past the guards. The turtles had a spinner pinned on the ground and the ambos were wheeling off a stiff to the meat wagon. Grant recognised the sheet-covered shape lying on the gurney. So did the others.

Grant felt a hand on his shoulder, and in his ear, 'Sorry, bra, Mad Dog didn't deserve dat.'

The spinner went to Katingal and Colin 'Mad Dog' Wilson was buried in the dirt out at Field of Mars. Colin had grown up as a houso in Gladesville.

'I assume he'll be going to hell then?' Grant asked the chaplain. Grant was angry, totally pissed off. Nothing was making sense – especially when the chaplain couldn't, or wouldn't, answer this simple question.

That night, Grant woke up in the midst of an indescribably disturbing dream to find himself whimpering like a baby animal. Darkness and hopelessness followed. His lethargy attracted the attention of a warden who alerted a doctor. The antidepressants didn't touch the sides and for the first time in a long time, Grant thought about scoring some drugs. Certainly, next time he was offered some pruno, he'd say yes. His new cellie, Nico, reckoned he could get onto some stuff.

He resisted the urge. Every time he thought about getting off his head, he thought about Mad Dog. He thought he'd be letting him down. He could hear Mad Dog saying, 'You won't be letting me down, son. You'd be letting yourself down.'

After missing a few weeks of music class, Grant returned. Muz and the boys in the class welcomed him with hugs and smiles and he was ushered over to the drum kit.

Everyone agreed it was perhaps the best way to work out some shit. 'Let it rip,' they called out. 'Give it some stick!'

Grant gave it his all. Arms belting, legs pumping. The others picked up instruments and joined in. It was chaotic, frenetic, madness of the greatest beauty. It went on for a good ten minutes when Grant, and he had no idea how he did this, but he began to slow down the beat so that everyone knew the song was ending. At the final crescendo, the whole class burst into uninhibited laughter.

Grant had turned a corner.

'Anything can go to shite,' Mad Dog would say, 'if you let it.'

Grant smiled whenever recalling his old mate's wisdoms. On the surface. they were a hybrid of new testament verses and prison survivalism, but in essence they were deeply human, forged inside a conscience dealing with the most horrible of tragedies.

Doing time drives most men mad. For a few, it's a gift. Something to be grateful for. A saviour. Now, Grant thought, let's get yourself out of here on your own two feet, son. Don't want to leave on a gurney.

Day five hundred and forty seven. Exit processing. Grant signs the paperwork and is handed a vacuum-packed bag with his clothes and possessions from day one. He undresses out of the prison greens and into civvies. He stands on the line and waits. Still, so much waiting. Easy, he thinks. Now an Opal card, now an envelope with $80 cash. He gets a two-man escort out through the gates and onto the street.

'See you soon,' heckles one of the guards.

Not a chance, thinks Grant as he holds his head high to breathe the salty air blowing in from off the bay.

X, Y and Z

Draft opinion piece: 3 March 2021.

We are simmering, it's obvious now. Simmering away in our own confusion of juices. There were warnings; rational, scientific, virtually irrefutable. Some of us fought for change. Battle after battle, inches gained, metres lost, measurement standards meaningless in the tower of Babel which our society had become.

Out at one end of the Faith in Humanity spectrum sit the conquered, who happily swallow the bitter pill of fate – humanity's fate, that is – whatever that may be. They have switched off from politics and feast on reality TV and home-delivered meals. Some of us try to persuade them to at least take a look at all the injustice. They justify their withdrawal from debate: 'That's the way it is. It's always been this way. It will all work itself out.' And they go off to work and buy lottery tickets.

On the other end, proud and crazy, stand those who have done their own research. They have switched off television, refused to vote, and immersed themselves into the esoteric worlds of enlightenment and conspiracy. They have connected the dots, and implore us to wake up. They dwell in cosy virtual chambers; they have found their tribe. They pity us, the scared sheep, yet they espouse the most frightening of scenarios.

Somewhere in the middle exists us, the normal folk, dare I use that term, who haven't got a clue what to do about it all.

Millsy is naked and asleep on the white PVC sofa in our lounge room. We took him in as a favour. Let sleeping dogs lie, they say. Though he is more like a bear: fat, hairy and snoring like some latent force of nature about to erupt. So, don't poke the bear, I guess.

Yuri wants me to wake him. She is worried he'll leave a human skid mark on the white three-seater we picked up from off the side of the road last Thursday. I remind her that we have no idea what sort or sweat or other fluid excretions had already been deposited onto its plastic surfaces by the previous owners over on Freeman Street.

'Can you disinfect it this time?' she asks in a whisper.

I nod and motion to Yuri to leave the room. I kick the sofa near Millsy's head. 'Wake up, mate!'

The snoring ends with a snort and the bear comes to life.

'You can't be nude in the lounge room, Millsy. And the sofa isn't for sleeping, you've got a bed for that.'

Millsy sits up. I imagine his sweaty date smearing itself along the fake leather. He looks at himself, startles at his own nakedness, and bolts down the hall to his room which is a curtained-off section of the closed-in veranda-cum-sunroom. Once a sparse light-filled area perfect for reading on a winter's day, now a dark cluttered cave. The only light is a freakish multicoloured LED glow that is emitted from his gaming computer set-up.

Millsy's mother deposits his share of the rent, plus an extra hundred dollars for miscellaneous expenses, each fortnight into Zoe's account. Zoe takes care of the bear's rent and withdraws the hundred dollars, which goes into the cash tin on top of the fridge. Zoe pays Millsy's share of the electricity, internet and streaming services out of her own pocket. As she says, 'It's the least I can do. It was me who persuaded you guys that we should take him in. Though I must admit I didn't know he was this much of a weirdo.'

Sharehousing, oh the joy!

'Thank you,' says Yuri as she watches me fetch the bleach-in-a-spray-bottle out from under the kitchen sink.

Yuri and Zoe went to school together; a Catholic systemic school up on the hill in the suburb where we all grew up. The Catholics had the best real estate and the parish priest drank the best wines. The condition of the school, though, was atrocious. I went there once for debating. I couldn't help but notice the flaking paint and cracked foundations. And I've never forgotten the stories about lesbian nuns wielding feather dusters with cane handles for discipline.

Yuri was the third speaker on the negative side of the debate that day and she whipped our public school arses. The topic, 'Public transport is taking us for a ride'. Stupidly, we argued, affirmatively, that of course it took us for a ride, that you get on at point A and off at point B. It didn't matter that the judge decided that our literal interpretation of the topic was naive and off point, the St Theresa girls were superior in every respect.

Riverview Boys High was, and still is, located in the humid lowlands. No breeze and no view of the river. But ultimately it doesn't matter where you do the HSC, or what you score, life is determined by a multitude of other factors, most of them way beyond one's personal control. Well, that is my hypothesis.

These days, you have to go to university no matter what you desire for a career. Problem is, careers are on the wane. Contracts and gigs are the new modus operandi given the so-called economic realities of employment. At uni, Yuri did political science, Zoe did arts and I did communications. Diplomat, arts administrator and journalist were our career choices. Now, graduates, none of us have permanent employment. We all work, but job security is a thing of the past, no matter what the Labor party says from opposition.

And the ACTU? I bumped into my old geography teacher from Riverview the other week. He was a staunch unionist back in the day. He always pre-empted his socialist rants with 'I'm not allowed to talk politics, but…' He's still teaching, these days just going through the motions, hating the piles and piles of bureaucracy that teachers get yoked with, looking forward to retirement, and glad as all fuck that he is on the old super system (Tracey, 2021). Yes, I have paraphrased.

'I pity you young folk today,' he said. 'How on earth you keep a positive attitude, I have no idea!'

The three-seater sofa gets a good wiping over. The bleachy smell restores some confidence in Yuri to be able to sit down and watch television later tonight. Yuri tells Zoe about the sleeping bear incident while we eat a dinner of pork stir fry, my night. Millsy consumes Ubereats in his cave.

Zoe is apologetic: 'Millsy's mum said it would only be temporary!' Who knows what that means.

'Temporary seems to be the current state of affairs for everything in this world,' says Yuri. 'Don't fret, Zo.'

I love Yuri. I love Zoe as well. And the reduced rent and extra hundred bucks a fortnight in the kitty, courtesy of Millsy's mum, is nothing to sneeze at. I'm a lucky man. I'm practising gratitude.

We clean up the kitchen together and debrief about our day. The bear cave is silent but a strange smell drifts down the hall. We all notice it. I volunteer to do something about it tomorrow. Zoe apologises again. Yuri wishes me luck.

It's eight-thirty and a Monday so we move into the lounge room to watch *Four Corners.* Thank God for the ABC, we all agree. There is hesitation among the three of us to sit on the now tainted sofa, so we agree to hold hands and lower our bums together.

'OK, on the count of three…'

We do it just as Lucy Carter introduces tonight's exposé. Coincidentally, the episode is about gaming and gamers.

I drift off in my mind, thinking about the draft opinion piece I scratched out earlier today. I am trying to understand the world. I have always been like this. And today I invented a spectrum, which I proposed was about faith in humanity. It is not the first time I have wondered about what people believe about the true nature of our own species. And it won't be the last. Are we innately good or evil? Immediately, I see the flaws in my post. My spectrum is not about this at all. It is about something else. I'm not sure what exactly. But I do know it is a reflection of my inability to understand how people can believe in some of the crazy conspiracy theories going around at the moment. And I have juxtaposed this against the people who I also don't understand, who don't seem to care at all about the way world works, or doesn't work – the mindless sheeple, as branded by the conspiracy theorists. It is a spectrum of sorts, a binary spectrum for sure, and I am acutely aware that those more intelligent than myself will outright reject this sort of over-simplistic theorising.

Millsy is supposedly on THE spectrum. The mother, Helen, claims the autism appeared a few days after his eighteen-month vaccination. Zoe's mother, who is Helen's second cousin once removed, or something like that, disputes this. She remembers Millsy before the jab. Apparently, Xavier Robert Mills never smiled, or crawled, or responded like a normal baby. Something was not quite right, she told Zoe. But never mind, you can't blame a mother for wanting a reason, an explanation, something or someone to blame for such misfortune. Zoe understands this, but raises her eyebrows at Helen Mills's stand on 5G, mask wearing, the deep state and Bill Gates. One night, Zoe showed us Helen's Facebook page.

'Fortunately, people with these views are in the minority,' said Yuri.

We love Yuri.

Four Corners ends with its iconic theme music that soothes my occasionally weary soul. There are fearless people still out there doing the hard journalism, and so far the government has not been able to privatise our ABC. I like to think that the people of Australia, weird or complacent as they can be, will never allow such a thing to happen. There's enough of us in the middle.

Zoe places her hand on my shoulder, 'If you want me to come with you when you confront Millsy tomorrow, I don't start work till eleven.'

April 2021

Friday, 2 April 2021

5.40 a.m.

The great Australian property bust – imagine it. Imagine all the investors whingeing their shiny arses off. Imagine all the blame and shame that would be cast about. Imagine the wealthy getting even richer from the bust while ordinary families suffer.

Have we reached peak narcissism?

A decade is a decent whack of time. Was the term narcissist being bandied around ten years ago? It certainly is nowadays. Every second person, and their fancy hybrid dog, seems to tick all the boxes to qualify for a clinical diagnosis of narcissistic personality disorder.

And is it any wonder why?

The modern world is dominated by laissez-faire capitalism, and the human race is getting bigger and more competitive. An equal share of the pie is rapidly shrinking by a simple law of mathematics.

To get ahead, to get a larger slice, one must run harder and faster with utmost confidence and the ability to lie and obfuscate and step on others to jostle one's self into a position of above-average comfort. No self-respecting member of the modern world would be content with average, so the story goes.

It's all about me. It's peak individualism. Me, me, me…

Thus the preponderance of the narcissist. And of every second person who is not a narcissist, most of them are classic enablers. They chide those few of us still left who possess a more collective vision of the how the world could be, as envious perpetrators of tall poppy syndrome.

Once, the most powerful person in the world was a narcissist. And some of his most hardcore supporters were the poor and downtrodden. His ability and audacity to bald-face lie was somehow ignored or excused by millions of voters. Meanwhile, there was a consensus amongst astute observers that the number one leader of the so-called free world was not only a narcissist, but a malignant one. A malignancy verging on psychopathy.

He is gone now, or is he? Is he in the wings – waiting, plotting, conspiring with his enablers to return with vengeance? Or has his toxic influence polluted the *zeitgeist* sufficiently that the era of unfettered individualism is destined to burn for another decade or two?

In the West, individualism is somehow equated with freedom and democracy. Western commentators like to point out how the rest of the world, the nations where perhaps a more collective world view is valued and legislated, is a world of human rights abuses and deprivation of freedom run by evil dictators. This grandiose propaganda is ubiquitous in Western media. And the fear it instils in the ordinary punter has us voting for right-wing governments time and time again, despite the immense weight of evidence showing the greed and corruption that pervades the so-called born-to-rule class of society.

In Australia, the popularised notion of 'having a go' has led to, among other injustices, a severe housing affordability issue. The insane current boom in real estate prices is dividing us further into a society of haves and have-nots. In the race to get ahead, the basic human need for shelter has become a pawn in the cruel game of private wealth creation. It seems that the initial hopes that the pandemic might cause a reset from rampant individualism to a more compassionate collectivism have vanished.

Will a bursting of the property bubble succeed where the pandemic failed? Will it be soon, or perhaps in a decade?

We watch and wait.

By Default

You've decided to do nothing this weekend. It was a hectic week. Next week will be worse according to middle management. Apparently, the Royal Commission into the Ineffectiveness of Royal Commissions has created a sense of panic in the upper echelons of the organisation you work for. You deliver essential services to the most needy in society. Once done by the public service, now privatised, you cling to the fact that your organisation is a not-for-profit, and thus, supposedly, by default, ethical. As you watch the CEO and the senior executives driving to and from work in BMWs, you cling ever tighter.

Sleeping-in on Saturday is impossible. It doesn't matter how late you postpone bedtime on Friday night, the Monday to Friday five a.m. alarm has conditioned your body clock. Recent talks by the 'staff welfare' branch of the HR department on how to establish and maintain a healthy work–life balance have you laughing under your breath. Obviously, work is not life, and HR know it.

The first sip of coffee is the best.

In your home office nook, you open up a fresh new Libre Office text document. It's not as satisfying as opening up the faintly lined first page of a brand-new exercise book, but it will do for today, Saturday. The default setting is A4, two-centimetre margins all round, single line spacing and you start typing full stops. Single keystrokes at first, one press for each full stop. Meditative in a way. After typing several lines, you hold the key down and watch the full stops appear magically, racing across the page, making line after line. Even at this pace, it will take quite a while to fill a full page.

Why are you doing this meaningless activity? Why not? You said you would do nothing this weekend. Just stop and recuperate. Holding a finger down on a computer keyboard is as close to doing nothing you can think of.

The second sip of coffee is not as satisfying as the first, but with all that full stop activity, the cup has cooled down somewhat, so you take a larger sip. Increased quantity to compensate for decreased quality. A metaphor for life? Or work?

The main benefit of word processors over exercise books has to be the editing features. Control A selects the half page of full stops. Control C copies it onto some ethereal clipboard in the virtual world inside your computer. Control V pastes the clipboard contents onto the page. Voila! You now have a full page of dots! Power at your fingertips. Well, actually, your select, copy and paste routine overshot the mark. You have two lines too many, there are dots on page two. Never mind, the backspace key takes care of that in a jiffy. No need for erasers, whiteout, or ugly striking out with the pen.

Full stops, dots, periods. English: why so many synonyms? The character count, again something not available on those old school analog exercise books, is eight thousand three hundred and twenty. You wonder if font makes a difference. Select all, change to Arial. The dots spill over onto page two. Font does matter. And so does font size. You go back to Times New Roman, font size 12, and zoom out to view a full page of eight thousand, three hundred and twenty dots. It's a lot of dots.

Now, with nothing else to do, and you committed to do nothing, you open your default web browser. It's Chrome, isn't it? And your home page, Google?

Chrome and Google aren't necessarily your favourites. Nor have you chosen them after careful consideration of all available options. But, for some reason which you aren't able to articulate, they have become your default settings. Microsoft would love you to use Edge and Bing. Avast, your free security software, somehow installed their browser onto your computer and you also have a version of Mozilla Firefox on there. You needed that when your community bank's online banking wouldn't load up on anything else. And how does one survive these days without online banking?

Remember the passbooks issued by banks? With deposits and withdrawals recorded by hand in blue ink by tellers. Remember banks when they were stand alone buildings in your town? Remember towns?

You remember now someone at work talking about how they only use DuckDuckGo for their search engine. They didn't want to be tracked. Mind you, they are an active user of Tinder, Facebook, Instagram and TikTok. And they crave attention. Some people!

You type in 'world population clock' and click on 'worldometers.info'. The human population on earth is ticking away faster than the seconds on a clock. You try to select the number with a click and drag; it doesn't work. You write it down with the pen and paper that sit next to your keyboard. The number you write down is immediately outdated. You round it up to the nearest hundred million. Seven point nine billion. It will get there soon, don't worry. Not even the latest variant of the latest virus is going to stem the exponential explosion of Homo sapiens on planet Earth.

After opening up the calculator app on your computer, you divide the world population by the number of fullstops on an A4 page. In other words, how much paper would you need to print a dot for each and every person.

949,519.23076923076923076923076923, rounded off – 950,000 pages.

Nearly a million. Now how many reams of paper is that? You know it's 500 sheets per ream. So, 950,00/500 = 1,900 reams. Back to Google, Google shopping now, reams are 297 centimetres wide x 210 deep x 55 high, 2.49 kilogrammes, and $4.99.

You imagine creating a modern work of art. An installation. The backdrop is a curved wall made with of reams of paper for bricks. It will be that pretty blue colour, Reflex blue. In front of this sits a small desk, facing into the wall of paper, on which sits an opened laptop computer displaying a page of full stops. The computer is attached to a home office inkjet printer, the kind you can buy at Kmart for less than the price of the replacement ink cartridges. There is also a stack of boxes containing those pricey little XL black ink cartridges. You couldn't be bothered at the moment calculating how many cartridges you will need to print out 7.9 billion full stops but it will be significant and perhaps the boxes of ink can also become a wall, a smaller wall, yes, and where you position it will depend on what space the gallery has allocated for your installation. The MONA in Hobart would love to have it, surely.

Now, the printing of the 7.9 billion dots is being performed by a boy and a girl, both naked, both nine years of age. This will cause a lot of controversy and outrage in the wider community. So much so that they may have to wear skin-coloured leotards, or better still, the boy and the girl could be androids, robots. Though budgetary considerations may dictate that real humans will have to be used. But then again, maybe robot children would cost less in the long run?

At the opening of your installation, which you haven't named yet – that will come – there is the obligatory arts crowd sipping Australian sparkling white wine and madly looking around at who is who in the zoo.

The gallery director introduces the piece with some bullshit speech. 'Blah, blah, blah...with regard to the issue of content, the subaqueous qualities of the facture visually and conceptually activates the exploration of montage elements. I find this work menacing yet playful because of the way the reductive quality of the consumerist motifs spatially undermines the essentially transitional quality...blah, blah, blah.'

You don't really care what he, or she, or ze says. It's all just a mind game. The wankier the better really. The crowd don't understand a word of what is said, mainly because it is meaningless drivel, but also because all their attention is on who has spotted them here at such a gala event. They applaud delicately, as you do with a champagne flute in one hand and an Apple watch strapped to the wrist of the other.

The two children now enter the installation and begin to print out the pages. There is a bin on one side of the desk for all the plastic packaging used for the ink cartridges. You know, the clear plastic bags that are a bugger to open, the peel-off protective strips, and the orange coloured twist-off plugs. On the other side of the desk is a paper shredder. Into that goes the glossy paper used to wrap the reams and also the A4 pages that don't print properly or get jammed and creased. The piles of shredded paper are burnt by the children in a brazier which provides them with heat and the ability to toast marshmallows on sticks for the necessary nourishment that is required for the duration of the project. The correctly printed pages are stacked in a semicircle on the floor in front of the set-up so that as the project continues the wall at the back diminishes and the wall in front grows to eventually conceal the whole useless operation.

How arty, you think. But really, you know it would fail. It is too literal, too obvious. Thanks to the likes of Koons and Hirst, you don't understand modern art at all and definitely don't have the money to employ other people to construct utterly meaningless garbage that the hoi polloi can fawn over and pretend to understand. You're no darling of the critics, that's for certain. In fact, you have no contacts in the art world at all.

The 'call to stool' gets you off the computer and onto the toilet. You could can your shit and display it as art. Though someone's already done it – 1961, actually. Sixty bloody years ago! So you'd be a copycat. I guess that's the trick: true art is doing something, it doesn't really matter what it is, just doing something that no one has ever done before. Duchamp turned a porcelain urinal into art all the way back in 1917. Is there anything that hasn't been done? Is 2021 just too late for anything new? Are we destined now to simply regurgitate and reinterpret the creativity of the great artists of the past? I mean, it has been said that all art is theft.

Hang on! You have an idea. You could start a whole new artistic movement where you retro what has already be retroed! It would be called Retroretroism, which would be described by the critics as the penultimate expression of post-postmodernism. Hang on? Has this already been done?

Your legs have gone dead. With elbows on knees, deep in thought, and defecation long finished, you have cut off circulation to the lower extremities. Your feet are numb, though strangely they feel thick and spongy.

After the rather prickly though joyous sensation of blood return, you stand up and proceed to wash your hands while singing happy birthday. A new habit. Who says you can't teach an old dog?

It's seven twenty-four a.m.

You go through the fridge and extract several cling-wrapped bowls with a selection of midweek leftovers and the last two eggs. Bubble and squeak. The default Saturday morning breakfast. As you eat it at the breakfast bench, you compile a shopping list on a piece of scrap paper, A4. You will go to the IGA in the old part of town. It's hanging in there. It's more expensive than the Coles, Woolworths and Aldi doing battle at the new shopping centre they built on the old wetland.

Remember wetlands?

On the way, you'll call in to see Aunty Flo. She'll make a pot of tea and offer you jam drops that she baked several days ago. You won't say no. Since Uncle Tom died, you've been helping her out with things around her house. You love that house. It's a time capsule of sorts. A small eddy, swirling around and around in the river of mayhem. Unaffected by the torrent of change sweeping through the world as we know it. You'll tell her how you are busy today, shopping and cleaning and doing a load of washing for yourself. But you will drop in tomorrow, open up Tom's shed, turn on the transistor, and in the wash of lazy Sunday radio you will potter about fixing whatever it is she needs.

'Don't forget to bring your shirts around,' she will say. And for the rest of next week, the citrusy smell of Fabulon on your collars will act as a protective barrier against the onslaught of well meaning work colleagues who are, by default, losing at Monopoly. The life-sized version of Monopoly, that is. The one that comes with real people, real streets and real plastic unaffordable houses.

Nobody irons like Aunty Flo.

And you said you would be doing nothing this weekend?

Tank and Ginger

The cake sits on the sideboard. The already opened chips and nuts slowly absorb moisture from the humid November air.

'Bugger it,' says Tank to himself. He grabs a handful of nuts, walks out to the esky on the back deck and retrieves a beer.

'What are you doing?' asks Ginger.

'Having a beer.'

'Shouldn't we wait?'

'They were meant to be here an hour ago. Stuff 'em!' He laughs and winks.

Ginger smiles and waves him on. Back in the kitchen, she turns the oven off and lets the potato bake sit in its own heat.

Tank is turning forty. 'Just family,' was his response when Ginger asked, weeks earlier, who he wanted to invite over for a Saturday birthday celebration.

Ginger's attempts to contact those coming to the barbecue-cum-birthday bash remain unanswered. She opens the news app on her phone. There has been a smash on the M1 near Mt White.

'Tank, there's a smash on the freeway. Again. They must be caught behind it. I wish they'd call.'

'Probably in a black spot.' Tank reaches into the esky and pulls out a can of vodka and fruit-flavoured soda. 'Here. They could be hours yet.'

'They said they were going to come in a convoy. You know how they are. I hope they're OK.' The vodka enters Ginger's bloodstream and dissolves a tension in her shoulders. Ethanol, the universal solvent.

Tank thinks about the convoy on the freeway. There would be Ginger's parents in the lead car. Bob driving, Helen riding shotgun. She'd be giving instructions and warnings. Tank doesn't know how Bob has put up with Helen for so many years, though she does iron Bob's clothes every morning and offers him whatever he wants for breakfast. But that voice, screechy and incessant. She gives a running commentary on the world. With his head inside the *Sydney Morning Herald*, or lost inside Classic FM on the car radio, Bob lives in some other world, unperturbed by Helen's voice-over.

Ginger's nothing like her mother.

Bob and Helen have an Audi. Top of the range. Bob makes buckets of money in his well pressed business shirts. Just don't ask him what he does. Nobody understands the answer he gives. Something to do with research and development in the third world. He is doing very well out of helping the less fortunate, supposedly.

Right behind the Audi, tailgating, will be Gerard. Gerard is Mandy's husband. Mandy is Ginger's big sister. Gerard will have cocaine. Gerard drives a massive LDV utility, his work truck. His penis extension. Everyone loves Gerard. He is upbeat, and is Mandy's saviour according to the family narrative. Though you have to give some credit to the mental health doctors and nurses who regularly review Mandy's medication and support her through the every-once-in-a-while ECT reset. Gerard and Mandy don't and won't have children. Probably a wise decision, thinks Tank.

Tank likes Gerard. Though he is superficial and has his eye on the father-in-law's estate, at least he's upfront about it. He can laugh at himself. The embarrassing story Gerard tells, anytime there's a chance, about the cosmetic surgery gone wrong, is something that Tank would definitely keep private. Not that Tank would ever have pectoral implants.

The kids, the next generation, are all in the third car. It's a bomby Mitsubishi Magna that was once, ten years ago at least, Helen's car. Daisy, Bailey and Leonard will be sitting three abreast on the back seat. They'll be pinching and poking each other.

Their mother, Georgina, will be feeding them fruit and trying to distract them from each other. 'Look at the river, kids. Remember when your pa hired that houseboat and we motored up to Berowra Waters.'

'Can we do that again?' asks Daisy, the eldest.

Her two younger brothers ignore their mother as they niggle each other.

Driving the Magna is Nick. Nick is a dick and everyone knows it. Nick has been trying to prove himself to his father for as long as anyone can remember. He is Helen and Bob's third child. Spoilt rotten. Two big sisters, a cashed-up father and a mother who mollycoddles him to this day. Currently, Nick is trying to make his millions by running a personal development company where he is the head life coach and mentor to a team of misfits he has trained to do online sessions with suckers willing to fork out hundreds of dollars in ongoing fees. Problem is, there aren't enough suckers or, more likely, too many life coaching services.

Helen is paying Nick's rent. It's just one of the many financial bailouts that have been gifted to Nick over the many years littered with a succession of failed hair-brained schemes. Bob would like to retire, but he is waiting for his grandkids to grow up. And he cares about Georgina. How his son ever landed himself a devoted and beautiful wife, he has no idea.

There's a family rumour that Bob is writing Nick out of his will. Georgina and the grandkids will be looked after, just Nick will be left out. Nobody questions why.

'I'm checking the telly.' Ginger gets up and heads inside.

Tank and Ginger can't have kids. After trying for many years, they made appointments with their respective doctors. Tank has a low sperm count and Ginger's Fallopian tubes are scarred. They agree it is probably not meant to be.

Tank has no real family of his own. He has numerous foster-parents, some good, some not so good. But they are all in Victoria, the state in which he was a ward until he bolted north at the age of sixteen. When Ginger watches Tank with the niece and nephews, she feels sorry that he will never have his own children. Tank shrugs it off in his usual unflappable and everything-will-be-fine manner. Ginger, when swamped by maternal hormones and desires, or reminded by well-meaning friends of her ticking biological clock, reconciles the situation by reflecting on the crazy dramas that regularly play out in her own family.

'Tank!'

'What?'

'Come here.'

The news helicopter footage shows a pile-up of cars and trucks just visible through heavy smoke.

Ginger is looking at the wrecks, looking for her family convoy. She touches the screen. 'Oh, my God! Look, Tank. Is that them?'

Tank leans in to check. It doesn't help; the resolution is what it is. Coming closer only reveals pixels. But it could be. Three of the dozen or so vehicles could be the convoy. Ginger grabs onto his arm, hiding her eyes into his bulk.

'When is this footage? It's not live, is it? Try calling again. Try Georgina. Or Daisy. She has a phone, doesn't she? Do you have her number?'

'Turn it off, Tank. I can't watch that.'

Ginger heads back outside. She sits down and starts working on her phone. Calling, texting. Mother, father, sister, brother-in-law, brother, sister-in-law, niece. Nothing.

Her head is spinning. They must be in the accident. She drops her phone to the ground. Holds her head and sobs. Tank embraces her. Holding her and holding back his own thoughts of disaster and death. That bloody freeway, he thinks.

'I'm sure they're OK. What did it say on the screen? Traffic backed up for ten kilometres. They'll be stuck in that for sure. I bet they're in a cutting with no signal.'

Ginger can't talk. Though she intentionally moved away up the coast to create some distance from her oddball family who all live in the same suburb, she can't bear the thought of losing them. Her mother and father, for all their faults, had still managed to raise Ginger with a kind of love that she explains came from the best of intentions. And when she met Tank, who has no family at all, she realised how lucky she was. The way Tank deals with her crazy brother and sister is enlightening to watch, and has been a great lesson for her. Tank exudes gratitude. When he said he only wanted family for his fortieth birthday party, essentially meaning her family, she had to admire how he'd embraced them all. Adopted them, unconditionally, for life.

They wait. Ginger picks up her phone occasionally to check the news app. There are reports of fatalities. Helicopters ferrying the critically injured up to John Hunter Hospital. Police opening up the contraflows. Hours needed to clear the logjam.

Tank brings out the nuts and chips. 'Best get something in your stomach.'

The steaks, sausages and chicken kebab skewers sit in the fridge. The salads remain under clingwrap on the dining table. The cake, baked and decorated by Ginger herself, a labour of love, sits ominously on the sideboard. The number four and number zero candles, perhaps never to be lit.

Meat can go in the freezer. Salads into plastic containers. But what about that cake? What if they're all dead. How will I ever be able to tell Tank that I'm pregnant?

The nuts and chips remain untouched. Absorbing the humid air. They will be binned if the party never happens.

What about the potato bake?

The things you think of.

They wait. What else can they do? On the deck, out the back. Each passing minute adding fuel to imaginings of horror and trauma. Twisted metal, torn flesh. How many cars did they say were involved?

Ginger jumps up with a start and heads back inside to the television. Tank follows.

Fifteen vehicles involved. Ten dead. Six in critical condition. Commentators already pointing out statistics, theorising causes and arguing points of contention.

Tank peruses the wide shots and other footage being screened. The convoy of family cars is nowhere to be seen. He points this out. Ginger notes that one of the cars in the wreckage is the same silver as the Audi.

Fully aware of the pointlessness of trying to allay fear with facts, Tank remarks, 'How many cars are that colour these days?'

What else can he say?

Ding…ding ding…ding. Ginger's mobile is outside. She rushes out. A succession of texts from Helen, Georgina, Mandy and Daisy. They are safe. They have been finally directed onto the old Pacific Highway. They'are sorry, they are going to be very late.

'Bloody hell, eh? That was bit of a worry. Guess the barbie's going to be dinner rather than lunch.'

Ginger walks over to her gentle giant of a husband and hugs him with all her might. Tears of relief and immense love for her husband run down her cheeks.

'Love you, darl,' he whispers in her ear. Tank opens the esky, takes out a beer and offers another vodka mixer to his wife.

She declines. She shouldn't have had one before. But she was keeping a secret. A secret she planned to reveal at the cutting of the cake. I'm pregnant. But she will tell Tank now. Tell him before the madness and mayhem of her family turning up and creating a crazy and beautiful mess of their house.

Happy birthday, Tank.

Tribe

It had rained all night and at times it felt like the wind gusts were going to rip off the iron roof. In the morning, Josie is in the kitchen, poaching eggs and listening to one of the local radio stations. The smell of toast is in the air.

In between the stock standard commercial radio songs and the annoying breakfast crew, who fake laugh at each other's stupid jokes, come reports of flash flooding, power outages and school closures.

Alexander enters the scene of domesticity. 'You're up early,' he says as he opens the refrigerator door.

'I have to go into the city. There's an important meeting today.'

With his head down peering into the labyrinth of tupperwared leftovers on the second shelf, Alexander rolls his eyes. I have to.... Not again, he thinks.

'I have to reduce my carbon footprint.'

'I have to eat less carbs.'

'I have to update my Instagram.'

'I have to go, it's family.'

And perhaps most annoying of all, 'I have to find my tribe.'

On this quest, Josie has joined and quit several environmental groups and other activist organisations, she has flip-flopped from right wing to left wing and back to right wing in terms of her political allegiances, has experimented with several expressions of sexuality and gender, and has sent her DNA off to Ancestry.com. She was once gluten intolerant, and once a vegan. Currently, she consumes as much animal protein as she can, and has decided her cravings for white bread are worth the slight bloating. The relationship with her dysfunctional family oscillates from addiction to total abstinence.

Alexander once fancied that he and Josie might become an item. When she answered the advertisement and came around for an interview, he couldn't keep his eyes off her. But as time went on and he discovered what a crazy mixed-up lost soul she was, her beauty faded. In fact, he thought that her fantastic good looks were probably her downfall. So many times now, when finding a new circle of friends, or some group she could join, her great enthusiasm would be shattered when some lecherous man, or woman, preyed upon her flagrant deliciousness.

Even though he tuts, or shakes his head, or rolls his eyes, always in private, at her annoying habits and eccentricities, Alexander cares for Josie. There is some beauty still left inside of her. He sees it from time to time. And he wishes her the best on her quest to find her tribe, or whatever it is she is looking for.

The sound of the en suite toilet flushing alerts both Josie and Alexander.

Valerie and Melody have the main bedroom, and thus the en suite. The couple are presently in the middle of one of their all too frequent fights that go on for three or four days before they sort stuff out and fall madly in love again. It's a pattern that Josie and Alexander are all too aware of. So the flushing toilet, this morning, is an alarm. WARNING! – an angry lesbian is about to bring their dark mood into the communal space of the kitchen.

Josie pops her toast back down. Someone has turned the brownness knob down again, so it will need a second dose. She will watch it closely. It wouldn't be worth burning it and stinking out the house. Not this morning. It's clearly an eggshell morning. Just watch the toast, keep my head down, eat breakfast and get out of the house, she thinks.

A blast of rain hammers the roof.

'I don't think you should be going out today,' says Alexander.

'I have to.'

'No, you don't.'

Valerie storms into the kitchen. The banging of the cupboard door after the swift extraction of her coffee canister puts an end to any hope of communal harmony. The violent filling of the kettle and the aggressive flicking of the power switch punctuate the scene with an exclamation mark.

'How can you two listen to this shit!' says Valerie about the morning radio show that is struggling to penetrate the storm both outside and in. She hits the preset button twice to shift the station to the ABC.

A sober voice reads out a list of road closures and relays a warning from the SES that people should stay at home and not venture out unless it absolutely necessary.

'If it's flooded, forget it.'

'Fuck!' screams Valerie.

Obviously, she needs to be somewhere. Who doesn't, thinks Alexander. Oh dear, thinks Josie.

Valerie storms out of the kitchen and back to her room, slamming the door behind her. There is muffled yelling – Valerie. And sobbing – Melody. Poor Melody, think Josie and Alexander in unison.

Once, Josie was jealous of Valerie and Melody. The lesbian couple seemed to be so happy and self-assured. Their sexual proclivities automatically assigned them a tribe. Josie even tried to join the LGBTQIA+ community by declaring herself pan-sexual and having a brief fling with a non-binary person named Kendall. But Kendall turned out to be even more lost than Josie. On top of that, this so-called community was riven by political factions and personal agendas. The whole scene was way too intense for Josie. Eventually, she decided that she was plain old heterosexual. Regardless, Josie has not given up her search to find her tribe.

'Come and have your eggs in my room. I'm just going to have this pawpaw.'

'Thanks, Alex.'

Inside the relative safety of Alexander's bedroom, he and Josie eat their breakfasts. In one corner is a television with the volume down low. They watch the scrolling news ticker. Trees are down in several places on the train line between Newcastle and Sydney. There are major and minor flood warnings up and down the whole of the east coast of NSW. It is a one-in-a-hundred-year event, the second one this autumn.

Valerie's car starts up in the driveway. Josie's and Alexander's shoulders relax and drop. Melody knocks on Alexander's door. She is invited in. She curls up on his bed. Nothing needs to be said. The car backs out and the angry revving and acceleration away down the street is quickly smothered by the sonic blanket of rain and wind.

Josie finishes her eggs on toast, places her plate on Alexander's dresser and wraps herself around Melody. They lie there, warm and dry, watching the drama unfold on the television. There will be no politics this morning, no updates on the vaccine roll-out, no live crosses to journalists outside courthouses, no film reviews and, best of all, no mention of the economy. It's all about the storm which is closing down the eastern seaboard of Australia.

Alexander finishes his pawpaw, picks up Josie's plate and heads out to the kitchen. Being now thirty-five years of age and having left home at seventeen, he is well adapted to share-house living, though would dearly love to have a place of his own. The desire peaks this morning. He recalls a few years ago now the long late-night conversations with Josie when she was ensconced in the local branch of the Labor Party. She was certain she had found her tribe. She was equally certain that there was a shift in public sentiment to the left. That the campaign to end negative gearing of residential properties would be widely supported and the key to ousting the presiding LNP government. She was wrong. And he was wrong. Houses are more expensive than ever. She said to him the day after the election loss, after the night where the party secretary of the local branch of the party put his hand on her backside, how glad she was that Alex was like a big brother to her, and how he would never do such a thing.

He rinses his and Josie's plate in the sink. It's as close as a couple as they will ever be. Alexander is fine with that. She is a lost soul; they could never really be happy together. She'll always be looking for her tribe.

The radio falls silent, the kitchen light goes dark with a tink.

Josie calls out from his bedroom, 'Alex, there's a blackout!'

Everyone did have to be somewhere that day. Valerie the only one to make it out. The others wonder quietly to themselves if she has got stuck somewhere. Has she driven into flood waters against all advice? Will she be on the news tonight being plucked from the roof of her car by a rescue worker dangling from a helicopter? That's if the power returns and the television can be watched.

If a car washes away in a flood and it can't be broadcast on the media, did it actually happen?

After resigning themselves to the fact that they should not and would not leave the house, the trio each have a shower while there is still hot water in the tank. Washed and warmed, they come together in the living room.

'Hot water on tap, the ultimate measure of civilisation,' suggests Josie.

'Is anyone getting any bars?' asks Melody holding up her mobile phone.

Alexander and Josie confirm the lack of signal.

No electricity, no internet, no phone. No light, no radio, no television, no heating, no refrigeration, no means of cooking. There are a few collective hours of battery charge on the mobile phones, laptops and various Bluetooth speakers owned by the household. Melody puts on the playlist of summer hits she compiled for Valerie's birthday last December. Music lifts the mood.

'I guess if the power doesn't come back on soon, we could cook on the gas barbecue,' says Alexander.

'You couldn't go out there now. You'd get soaked,' says Melody.

'That's if you weren't blown away first,' adds Josie.

'Hang on. The gas bottle's empty,' says Melody. 'Valerie cooked some haloumi on it last week and it ran out halfway through. I told her to get a refill. Sorry.'

'Don't be sorry, Mel. It's not your fault. You're not responsible for

Valerie. Anyway, we've got enough food that doesn't need cooking or heating up. We'll be fine,' says Alexander, always positive.

Josie excuses herself from the living room to go and read a book in bed. Alexander and Melody talk for a while. Nothing serious. House-mate chit-chat. When that runs out, they also retire to their rooms.

The day wears on. Josie has missed her choir meeting in the city. Alexander is not at work. Melody would have been at uni in Newcastle, but then again maybe she wouldn't have. She struggles to attend at the best of times, even in the fairest weather. Valerie is out there somewhere on her way to her work at the women's refuge. It's unlikely she got there, and it's a blessing she hasn't made it back home to terrorise her housemates with her bullish ways.

There is a banging on the front door. All three housemates attend. A petite woman dressed in baggy orange fluoro and big boots stands confidently with hands on hips.

'You need to be prepared to evacuate. The lake is rising.'

Josie recognises her from years ago at school.

'Where do we go? And how will we know when to go? We don't have any electricity and the mobile networks are down,' asks Alexander.

'Ideally, you should have a radio with batteries. So, the evacuation centre is at the community centre in Oaks Avenue and maybe you should head up there now.'

'Really, is it that bad?' asks Melody.

'It's not looking good. OK, what I'll do is head off up the road to tell more people and then I'll swing back and escort you up there if you want. Grab your most important personal effects, and a change of socks and undies. Whatever you can get in one bag.'

Josie remembers now. It is Angie Whitehall, the shy one in year eight who was constantly bullied until the day her mother interrupted a full school assembly on the quadrangle and screamed blue murder at the principal up on the rostrum. No one ever knew what happened to Angie, where she went, or how she felt about her mother's antics. She never did show her face again, at least not at Tumbi Umbi High School.

Josie steps forward. 'You're Angie, aren't you?'

'Yeah. Hi, Josie. How are you?'

The two old schoolmates chat on. Well, they were sort of mates. Josie always felt sorry for Angie and sat next to her in maths and science classes. But she didn't have the courage to hang out with her in the playground, where she was harassed on a daily basis.

Melody and Alexander excuse themselves and head back to their rooms to pack a bag as instructed.

Angie explains how her mother home schooled her up to year 10 and then how she went to a school in Sydney for year 11 and 12. She studied chemistry at uni and got a job at the Sanitarium food plant over at Chittaway. She has a husband and two young boys of her own. She volunteers for the State Emergency Service, where her mother is captain.

'And I did jujitsu, which came in handy more than once or twice,' says Angie with a smile that fills Josie with a strange reminiscent warmth.

A young man, also in fluoro and boots, calls out for Angie to get a move on.

'Gotta go. I'll swing by later.'

Josie closes the door and goes to pack a bag. A yelled-out conversation starts up between the bedrooms.

'What are you packing, Josie?'

'Do you really think we'll have to evacuate?'

'Shit! I can't find my passport.'

'Who do you reckon would have a battery-powered radio these days!'

'How do you know that girl, Josie?'

There is knocking at the front door again. Again, all three attend.

It's Old Mate from up the road. The one with the cane and the three-legged cattle dog who yells out, 'Hoi!' at the yobbos who drive V8 utes at high speed up their normally quiet suburban street. He sells vegetable and herb seedlings from under a gazebo he has set up in his driveway. Alexander talks to him from time to time and knows that he moved to Long Jetty from Sydney back in the seventies and was a builder and that his wife died of tongue cancer twelve years ago. But he doesn't know his name, so he is Old Mate.

'The young lassie from the SES said you don't have a tranny,' and he holds forth a radio, an old-school silver thing housed in a brown leather case. 'I've tuned it into the local ABC. They're giving regular updates.'

The trio thank their neighbour and he heads off back up the road.

Soon after, the door is knocking again. This time it's the smiley fellow from across the street. The one with the electric mower who appears to have a different girlfriend every month. Valerie noticed that. Valerie reckons he's a philanderer, a misogynistic philanderer no doubt. But Valerie isn't home today, thankfully.

'Hi, I'm Paul. From over there.' He points to his cottage with the well maintained front yard.

'Yes, hello. I'm Alexander, and this is Josie, and this is Melody.'

Paul invites them over for a hot meal. Noticing the surprised looks, he explains, 'I have gas.'

The housemates accept and, after getting their coats and Josie putting a note on the door for Angie, they follow Paul back to his house. Inside, the air is warm and filled with the homely aromas of cooking.

Josie notices an electric light above the stove. 'Is your power on?' she asks.

Paul explains how he is experimenting with some solar panels and batteries that he has set up himself. 'I'm still on the grid, and this twelve-volt system is just a backup, for situations like this.'

The group sit down for a bowl of chicken and vegetable curry served on jasmine rice. Paul asks about the other girl. He says he saw her take off in a hurry this morning.

So Paul is watching Valerie as Valerie watches Paul, thinks Melody.

'That was Valerie. She's my girlfriend. She took off in a hurry when she heard the roads might be closed. She's bit of a workaholic. Do you have a girlfriend, Paul?'

'Funny you ask that. I'm actually gay. My boyfriend lives in Melbourne for his work. I get down there as much as I can, but lately, as we all know, things have been a bit tricky.'

Bloody Valerie, thinks Melody.

The getting to know each other conversations continue. Paul is the eldest sibling in his family and has seven sisters. They visit often.

Josie reveals how she has only one brother, a junkie who she lends money to, against the advice of all others. 'I have to, he's my brother.'

Alexander restrains an eye roll.

Melody tells her story of coming out as a lesbian.

Alexander restrains another eye roll. He's heard this story before, several times. Melody was arranged to marry a man she had never met who lived in India. When she turned sixteen and passports and airline tickets were being sorted for the whole family to fly to Delhi for the necessary preparations, Melody brought Kimberly, her girlfriend at the time, home to meet the family. While everyone was sitting around the dinner table, Melody made a show of kissing Kimberly on the mouth and announced to her devout Hindu mother and father that she was a lesbian and there was no way in a thousand lifetimes she was ever going to marry a man, let alone marry anyone who she wouldn't meet until the wedding day! Poor Kimberly, thought Alexander when he first heard the story. Needless to say, Kimberly didn't last too long after that. Within a couple of years, Melody was banished forever from her family and she changed her name from Mitali Pradesh to Melody Pussycat. Yes, seriously.

When Josie went through her sexual identity crisis and tagged along with Melody and Valerie to countless dance parties and other queer-only events, Alexander felt quite left out and alone in the house which he himself had organised. There he was, white and male and straight, feeling awkward and alien in the prevailing *zeitgeist*.

Melody wraps up her recount and in the same breath asks, 'What about you, Alex? Tell us your story. Come on, it's about time you told us about your family.'

'As I've said before, Melody, you lot are my family. I mean it.'

'Come on,' Melody persists.

'I'm an orphan, OK?'

'Really?'

'Well, sort of. It's complicated.'

Catching on, Melody sits back in her chair and mouths a silent sorry to Alexander. Josie reaches across the table and squeezes his hand. She knows his story. Knows why he wouldn't want to share it, especially now, sitting at the dining table in the man-across-the-street's house.

Paul asks who wants dessert. He's done a bread and butter pudding in the gas oven. The aroma of cinnamon now makes sense.

After the meal, the trio head back home across the road. The rain has abated. Angie has written on the note left by Josie. It is her mobile number and an invitation to call if they need anything. Anything is underlined.

Inside, they chat about the kindness of their neighbours and how they had been so wrong about them. Melody confesses how she always thought Old Mate from up the road was a mean ol' cranky bastard. Josie expresses her delight at how things had turned out for Angie, and how she wished she had stood up for her back in year 8.

'And what about Paul? So all those women are his sisters! What a crack-up! Wait till Valerie finds out.'

The mention of Valerie elicits a pause.

'Hey, guys,' says Melody, 'I'm really sorry about me and Valerie fighting so much lately. I don't know what to do. She's so touchy about stuff. I feel like I'm walking on eggshells.'

'It's OK, Melody,' says Josie, reaching across and touching her forearm, 'I'm going to have a chat with her. I've decided. Enough is enough. We are a family, you're right, Alex. I mean I love her, but she needs to think about her effect on others. To be honest, I'm scared of her, and that's wrong. Yes. I'm going to talk to her.'

The sound of a car: the motor, the brakes, the handbrake, the dying of the motor, the opening and closing of the driver-side door, unmistakably Valerie.

The housemates are sitting around the dining table dressed in beanies and blankets. The old-school radio which Valerie has never seen before sits in the centre broadcasting. Finally, some good news: the east coast low is abating.

'Hi,' says Valerie, looking down at her feet.

'Hi,' is the reply in unison.

'I have to say something. To all of you actually, but mostly to you, Melody. I've been a real bitch lately. And I'm sorry.'

Valerie looks up from the floor to see her lover and two housemates looking back at her. Are they faces of disbelief? worries Valerie. No, they are faces of relief.

'Yes,' says Josie. 'You've been a right royal bitch! Get over here and give us all a big hug. A group hug! We haven't had one of those for a while.'

After the reconnection and further apologising from Valerie, and expressions of love and understanding from her household, Valerie asks about the radio. Alexander explains.

'Really? You mean Old Mate?' Valerie appears genuinely surprised.

'Yes. And we had lunch with Paul across the road,' says Melody.

'Nooo. Did he have a lady friend there?'

'No,' says Josie. 'Paul's gay. All those women are his sisters.'

'Nooo.' Valerie extracts herself from the group circle and sits down at the dining table. She hides her face in her hands. 'God, I've been a dick.'

They all know Valerie's story. It's not a pretty one. Years of childhood sexual abuse from a stepfather, which to this day, despite the very public court case and conviction, is denied by her mother.

Melody sits down beside Valerie and puts her hand on her lap. Alexander and Josie place a palm each on Valerie's shoulders.

Many hands make light work, and at the laying on of hands the electricity switches back on. The kitchen light and radio come to life. The cadence of the ABC radio continues with its community service of storm updates.

Valerie extracts herself from the comforting hands, stands up and heads over to the electric radio. She presses the preset button to change the station to the local commercial station, which is playing a well worn cheesy pop hit. She begins to dance. The others join in. They form a circle facing in towards each other. They stomp feet, raise hands and sing out the melody with la la las as no one knows the lyrics.

The east coast low is abating, outside and in.

Josie is dreaming. She is inside a convention centre filled with rows and rows of stalls representing political parties, sporting teams, religious congregations, activist groups, ethnic societies, dance schools, talent agencies, fan clubs, organic food collectives, wealth creation consortiums, fitness organisations, art associations, gambling syndicates, to name a few. Everywhere, teardrop banners and video screens assault the senses. Trestle tables are crammed with tote bags pre-filled with discount vouchers, coffee mugs, lanyards, promotional pens and rubber wrist bands. Then there's the onslaught of spruikers, men and women dressed and groomed immaculate. They compete to catch Josie's eyes and beckon her to enter their pop-up modular cocoons.

Welcome. Join us. Take a seat. Happiness and belonging await. Sign up now! Just leave your email address. Here, have a tote bag.

Every fear she's ever had swirls inside her. She wants to run. To escape the mania. But she can't run. Her legs won't work. She tosses and turns and drenches her bed sheets with a storm of night sweat.

A hand touches her shoulder. She turns to see a mob. Up front are Alexander, Valerie, Melody, Old Mate from up the road with his three legged dog on a leash, Paul from across the road, and Angie still in her boots and fluoro uniform. Around them are more people. There's the lady from the post office and the bloke who collects the plastic bottles out of people's recycle bins. There's the barista from the Obsidian Tambourine and the women who runs boot camp on the headland above the beach.

The exhibition hall has vanished. They are down by the lake, pelicans flying overhead and cyclists passing by and dinging their bells. Josie can smell doughnuts and coffee. A band plays music from a stage on the shoreline.

'Josie,' a voice calls. There is a figure out on the jetty holding a rope connected to the bow of a bobbing boat. He calls out again, 'Josie! I can take you to the city. Come now.'

The crowd disappears. The music stops. There is only the person holding the boat and a sulphurous smell of lake sludge. Josie walks out onto the jetty. There are planks missing and she has to step over the gaps which get wider and wider as she proceeds.

'That's it. You're nearly here. Keep coming. Everything will be all right,' calls the figure.

Josie comes to a gap so wide she will have to jump. The water on the lake is choppy and splashing up onto the planks making them slippery. She stands at the gap. The person with the boat beckons her on. She can see their face now. It is familiar. It is a composite face of all the people who have conned her, flattered her, condescended her, touched her.

Another voice calls from the shore behind her, 'Josie!'

As she turns her feet slip and she loses balance. Falling back. Back into the gap.

She falls into her bed. Wakes in fright in her bed of twisted sheets and sodden pillows. She gasps for air. Realises it was all a dream. She is safe now. Home. Her breathing eases.

The smell of toast is in the air. The en suite toilet flushes. Cars pass in the street. Her tribe begins another day.

www.ingramcontent.com/pod-product-compliance
Lightning Source LLC
Chambersburg PA
CBHW051231210726
48290CB00003B/911
9781761094002